AT THE END OF THE WORLD

EROTIC STORIES

CHRISTIAN PAN

AT THE END OF THE WORLD

First Edition: December 2022

Formatted by: Colorful Pen Press
Cover Designer: Tatiana von Tauber

For E.,
Lord of the Barflies

DRESS TO GET LAID

I don't even remember his name, as it was so many years ago and I was drinking so fucking much back then. So, let's just call him Jeff.

"I mean, what the fuck are we even *doing* in Iraq?" Jeff was asking me—no, shouting at me, really—while simultaneously taking another gulp from his pint of beer. "I mean, none of the hijackers were even Iraqi," he intoned somberly, as if this fact made a lick of difference.

The two of us were sitting in the corner booth of a tiny bar on our quaint little college campus, somewhere in New England. Once upon a time, the place was really freewheelin´ and wild. Everyone seems to think the place is just one giant orgy, but I think those days (or nights) ended just before I enrolled there. Still, compared to other small liberal arts colleges, I guess this place was a bit more loose or extreme than most of its academic neighbors in the Green Mountain State.

My fourth plastic cup of cheap red wine stood motionless between my hands on the wooden table. My

1

cup looked significantly smaller than Jeff's pint of Anchor Steam. Why was his drink in a glass, and mine in plastic?

Deep thoughts. From the mind of a drunk.

Not that I was able to admit it to myself. Not then.

"As a student of the theater, I think this whole thing with Iraq is all very… Shakespearean," I pronounced, swigging the last of my drink. "The Son. Trying to prove something to….The Daddy. There's this whole…take over the throne thing. A plague on both houses. Etcetera, and so on, ad infinitum."

Jeff looked at me over the edge of his beer, which had stopped short of his mouth, and frowned. "What Shakespeare play are you referring to, dude?"

"Any of them," I said dismissively. "All of them. I mean, they're all infused with that, y'know, *subtext*."

After a beat, we both laughed. And then, we just silently drank some more, communing with our thoughts. Jeff was all right. Both of us were cognizant that we hardly knew each other. But neither of us wanted to be drinking alone tonight.

"Operation Iraqi Freedom," he snorted.

"Right? How much of our taxes went into paying people to come up with *that* shit?"

"I mean, why wasn't there any investigation into the attacks? When that plane went down over Lockerbie, they, like, *salvaged* all of the wreckage they could find from the bottom of the fucking *ocean*. To study it, make sure something like that never happens again. You know? But with the Towers? Just threw it all away, as fast as possible. What the *hell*, y'know?"

"Whoa!, easy, bin Laden," I said, doing my best Texan drawl. "Sounds like yer sympathizin´ with them thar *terrorists!*"

"Fuck off."

Jeff drained his beer then slid out of the booth. He held the empty glass towards me, and I nodded. I´d get the next round, but I hoped something happened soon. The drinks were making me restless.

I looked around the bar. The place was empty except for me, Jeff, and Ben, the bartender. He always seemed surprised whenever we'd come up to him with our money, that he had to put down whatever book he was reading and actually pour us a couple of drinks. *The Marshall Mathers LP* was playing from the speakers that hung suspended in the corners of the place, because Ben wanted the world to listen to Eminem's musical catalog in sequence before enjoying his latest release, which he promised to play tonight. Whoopee.

Jeff returned to the corner booth, placed the new drinks on the table between us, then slid onto the seat across from me. He smiled, took a sip, then placed the glass down. His head began nodding in rhythm to "Stan," and kept nodding as he looked around the bar as if just seeing it for the first time. "Hey. Where the fuck *is* everybody?"

As if on cue, a couple of cute Freshman girls took three steps into the bar. They looked at me and Jeff, then at each other, then made a sharp U-turn. I could hear them giggling before the metal door slammed shut behind them.

I looked at him, and realized Jeff´s question was one hundred percent genuine. "What´s today?"

"Saturday," he said, shrugging his shoulders. "So?"

I shook my head wearily, the weight of invisible and

inarticulate burdens heavy on my heart. "Dress to Get Laid."

"Ohhhhh!" Jeff brought his palm to his forehead. He made too big of a show of appearing like he forgot, but he did his best. I guess I wasn't that drunk yet. "That's tonight?"

Practically every week, the College hosted some kind of theme party. Most of them seemed pretty lame, but there was one that seemed popular with every sector of our remote little campus, one which helped keep our rep as a wild and crazy place intact: this was the "Dress to Get Laid" party.

This party was the one each semester where the inmates really got to run the asylum, at least in theory, and the College basically turned a blind eye to it. Maybe they figured that the kids were gonna do it anyway, so why not try to keep it relatively supervised? Basically, a bunch of students at Dewey hired a DJ, bought a couple of kegs, and invited everyone to come dressed up in something really really sexy. Combined with dimming the lights, cranking up the music, and having lots of alcohol, the hope was that everyone who attended would get lucky.

Not that different from *any* night on *any* college campus, I guess. Only here, with students largely coming from trust funds, there was a little extra snark, an added dose of irreverence and sarcasm about the whole thing. People really got into the dressing up, and I hoped everyone found whatever it was that they were looking for. Personally, I think everyone who went to a party called Dress to Get Laid was pretty fucking insecure, as if their clothes would camouflage how needy they felt, as if

4

wanting some companionship for the night was too hard to ask for. Most of the students were barely older than high school kids, after all. Their brains were still forming.

Like I was one to talk. Even though I was in the graduate program, I didn't have the balls to show up there during the four semesters I´d been at this place. I had little cash, and what money I had I spent on booze instead of some kinky Halloween costume. I mean, what the fuck? Was I gonna just show up there in my jeans and a tee-shirt? Rather than get rejected by some twenty-something, I´d rather just get a bottle and drink. Just pretend to be too cool, too above it all, or whatever. Instead of actually trying my luck at a place where everyone was basically horny, I´d just slither over to the campus bar and have a couple of drinks. See what was happening. Talk with Jeff, or his equivalent.

Jeff. Poor guy. Was he *really* unaware of the party? I squinted into his face, looking for answers. His skin was pale, so I deduced that he spent his free time in the goddamn library, staring at screens beneath fluorescent lighting. What was his major again? I think he already told me. Did he have any friends? I wondered if Jeff had ever had sex before. I lifted my plastic cup and mused.

"Yeah," I said, hoping this mouthful would at least get me drunk. "I think the party started a couple of hours ago."

"Why aren't you there?"

I shrugged, smiled, and deflected. "I don't know," I replied. "Why aren't *you* there?"

"Come on," he said, "I´m a *first* year. Plus a *transfer*. I barely know anybody yet. You´re a *grad* student, who's been here nearly two years already."

Two years? Jesus fucking Christ.

"You know people," he continued. He lifted his pint glass, then put it down without taking a sip from it. After a pause, he added. "Besides. You´re better looking."

I raised an eyebrow. "Are you coming on to me?"

Jeff blushed, then quickly swallowed a mouthful of beer. It looked like he was going to say something, but before he could answer, Catherine walked in. And she was pissed.

Now, even though this was many many blackouts ago, I have no problem remembering *her* name. Catherine was a junior, and totally fuckin´ hot. Skin paler than porcelain. Straight black hair, falling all the way down to her waist. Nice big tits. And an ass I could just sink my face into. We ´d had maybe half a dozen interactions before, always at a party, as we obviously didn't have any classes together. I remember we always ended up talking about Scotland and Ireland. She was all about Gaelic ancestry, druids and bagpipes and shit, which we had in common. I sensed that there *might* be something there with Catherine, if I ever wanted to pursue, but I always chickened out. Being thirty-one and her being twenty or twenty-one, I felt old and out of the loop. Sure, we could talk about Edinburgh or whatever, but it seemed trite. So, after talking with her for a few minutes at whatever campus party we'd see each other at, I ended up drifting away before the conversation ran out of gas, and she'd find someone new to talk to.

I'm such a catch, right?

Anyway. Tonight, Catherine came bursting into the campus bar in a fury. She was dressed like a college student´s idea of a dominatrix, and it was definitely working for her. The black corset she was wearing was a great choice, in my opinion, as it emphasized her naturally large chest, which bounced with every click click click of her high-heeled boots that laced up all the way to above her knees. Her black leather skirt just barely covered her hips, and I was tempted to lean sideways out of the booth to get a better look at her ass, see if I could sneak a peek.

Still fuming, she made a beeline for our table once she saw me. She threw down the purse that had been slung around one bare shoulder, a bag large enough to contain a single package of cigarettes and maybe a pair of keys. She slid into the booth next to me, and when I smelled the sweat coming off of her forehead, I felt an erection begin to stir between my legs.

"Aaargh!" she groaned. She placed her palms onto the sides of her head, framing her face like that trippy Munch painting. Then, she got out of the booth, marched over to Ben, and then demanded a cup of wine. I watched the little drama unfold. Even though I couldn't make out any specific dialogue because of the Eminem soundtrack, their body language told me the story. No matter how much Catherine flailed and gesticulated with her hands, Ben just kept slowly shaking his head left and right. Finally, she placed a hand on her hip, and let out a sigh big enough to fill the room, and even to cut through the music for a moment. Ben laughed, nodded, and poured her some kind of soda from the gun behind the bar. She took a sip, shot him a vengeful stare, then skulked back to me, or maybe she just wanted to keep an eye on her purse. With one hand, Catherine shooed me closer to the wall before flopping down beside me, her breasts jiggling inside her corset..

"Fuckin' *shite!*" she said. She stirred her soda before tossing the straw onto the center of the wooden table. Catherine was from Georgia, not Glasgow, but whenever she got high or tipsy, I noticed a faint lilt creep into her speech. Like her wannabe dominatrix outfit, though, this affected accent worked for her.

"What's up, lassie?" I jabbed, playing along with my best brogue. "Hard day at the dungeon?"

She gave me the finger, then snubbed me by explaining to Jeff, "What's a pretty girl gotta do to get a fookin' *drink* around here!"

"Aren't you twenty-one?" I asked.

She turned to me, and batted her eyelashes. "Next month, darlin'," she said, suddenly Southern.

Smooth as a Vegas card-dealer, I switched her Coke for my half-filled plastic cup of cheap-ass red wine. "Quick," I whispered. "Now's your chance. Before Ben sees you."

Catherine didn't need to be prodded. She promptly finished my drink in one gulp.

"Oy! I said a *sip,* ya wench."

She flashed her smile, her white teeth now faintly stained pink. Catherine then gave me a quick peck on the cheek, her lips making my skin feel like it was glowing red, and reminding me that this girl could get away with murder (with me, anyway). She adjusted her corset to make sure her tits were not falling out. Or maybe she was just reminding the boys at the table that she *had* tits, great ones, in fact. Not that Jeff or I had any doubts about her voluptuous femininity. Fixing her costume to her satisfaction, Catherine looked around and gave us her next proclamation in her normal voice. "You all have

8

the right idea, being here," she said, looking across the table at Jeff.

"Wh-what do you mean," he chuckled nervously. I could be wrong, but I think I was witnessing the first time Jeff ever had a girl engage him in actual, direct conversation. Or maybe he was stuttering because Catherine´s wonderfully big bust was distracting him.

"That Dress to Get Laid party? *All women!*" Catherine put her head into her hands. "I mean….*bloody hell!*"

I turned to Jeff, and raised the cup of Coke. "Looks like we´re at the wrong establishment, mate. What say we finish up here, and--".

"Oh no no no no," Catherine said, elbowing me in the ribs, and then giving the top of my thigh a squeeze. "You ´re staying right here. With me. At least until we finish our drinks."

I smiled. The night had suddenly gotten a lot more interesting.

"Well, you already finished *mine*," I said. "Move over. Let me get you another round."

Another kiss on my cheek before she slid out of the booth to let me pass. I was on my feet and across to the bar before you could spell *whipped*. When I came back, I bumped her shoulder with my hip so that she moved in closer towards the wall. I took one small sip of the wine before placing it in front of her.

"Who was there," Jeff asked innocently. "Anyone I know?"

Catherine wrinkled her forehead when she replied to him. "I don't know. Who do you know?" She took another sip of my wine, and then switched our drinks back with a wink. What a sweetheart. She ran her fingers through her long hair, and I appreciated the cheekbones of her profile. "I'm sorry," she said. "I'm being a real bitch--".

"Yeah, you are," I said, earning myself another elbow to the ribs. This one was harder than the first one. I laughed.

"It's just that I was looking forward to this party," Catherine whined, "got myself all dressed up….".

As she spoke, she traced the top of her chest with her dark red fingernails, outlining her flesh just below her collarbones, one of the most beautiful areas on a woman's body. Jeff was more obvious about it, but both of us had basically transformed into two dogs, panting and with our tongues hanging out. And Catherine´s smile told me that she knew the kind of effect she was having on us. And that she loved it. I mean, if she told us that we were going to rob banks tonight, we wouldn't have blinked. We probably would've fought over whose car we were taking, or who was going to drive.

Catherine changed roles again. This time, she did a pretty good impression of Marilyn, all fluttering eyelashes and tilting of her head when she asked, "So? What do you boys think we should do tonight to have fun?"

Jeff coughed, clearing his throat like a desperate salesman. "Well, um, I have a bottle of wine at my place."

Catherine smiled.

"I´ve got some pot," I said.

Her smile widened even more.

"And I don't have a roommate," she said, flicking her eyebrows up.

"Now we´re talkin´," I replied. I then switched back to the brogue: "So what the *fook* we still doin´ *here,* ay?"

Catherine laughed, and playfully pushed my shoulder to get me out of the booth. She was already heading towards the door with me trailing behind her, leaving Jeff to chug down the last of his beer. She paused briefly at the door, and motioned for us to follow with her index finger.

"Come on, boys," she said. "Let's make our *own* fucking party."

———

FIFTEEN MINUTES LATER, I hustled down the stairs from my dorm room at Franklin. The three of us had split up in the middle of the Commons Lawn, Catherine reminding us of our assignments of what to bring back to her room at Swan. In the darkness, Jeff bolted away to get more booze. I had been inside my place for less than a minute, before coming back downstairs. Tucked into two pockets were a ziploc bag of pot, courtesy of my dealer in New York, and all the condoms I could find. I felt like he and I were still acting like a couple of hounds, hoping to get back to Catherine's room first, maybe get a treat.

I looked south, past the Lawn, to what everyone on campus called the End of the World. I took a deep breath in, and chuckled. *What a night this one's turning out to be.* Heading towards Swan House, I saw a figure emerging from the front of Kilpatrick, his arm cradling a wine bottle like a baby. Jeff. Our trajectories were going to overlap en route to Catherine's place like two balls on a pool table. From Dewey House nearby, the Dress to Get Laid party seemed to be going strong, based on the music. The DJ they had hired had good taste: the extended remix of "Erotic City" was now seamlessly shifting into the teaches of Peaches just as I caught up with Jeff, who I greeted with a nod. Did any guys show up yet? Or maybe

Dewey had just become a Sappho Party? At this College, it wouldn't be beyond the realm of possibility for everyone to just embrace the fact that there were no guys around, and have a great time anyway.

I don't remember Jeff or me saying anything as we approached Swan House, where most of the windows were dark. Our feet trampled through the frosted grass, and I enjoyed the soft crunch of its sound. The crisp night air felt like adventure.

Five minutes and who knows how many fantasies later, the two of us stood at the threshold of Catherine's second floor dorm room, bearing our tributes to the domme. The College's residence halls for students were converted from traditional New England colonial houses, and each one looked pretty modest and simple from the outside. She kept hers clean and orderly. I liked how she had lit a bunch of candles around the place while waiting for Jeff and me to get there, nice ambience on a student budget. Catherine was cool and, I don't know why, but that little detail about the candles just made me grow more sweet on her. And horny. Giant posters of Siouxsie Sioux and Robert Smith watched over the room like pale deities, and the unmistakable voice of Andrew Eldritch, purring about the heat of the night, felt like an incantation.

The domme was still dressed to get laid as she welcomed us into her dim lair with a flourish. Three mismatched cups swiped from the dining hall were on a small glass end table, ready for wine. While Jeff went straight for the corkscrew, I took my time to look at Catherine. I was delighted to see she hadn't changed out of her black corset or thigh-high black boots, and I imagined licking her body as I rolled a joint with some paper. She sat with her legs crossed on the sofa, which had become her throne for the night, and her right ankle flexed in time to the beat of the song. I liked how her large breasts expanded whenever she breathed in. Catherine's corset barely covered her bust, and I couldn't wait to see them liberated. I was wondering what color her nipples were when she caught me staring. I felt myself blush, tried to keep looking at her, but I was the one who looked away first.

"How's it going over there?" she asked Jeff, as if he were a child. He seemed to be having trouble getting the bottle open. *What the fuck, man? Is this the first night you've ever had booze, too?* Suddenly, a loud pop, and we all exhaled. The bottle barely got to breathe before he began to pour.

"Sorry about that," he chuckled. He bent his body over the table to fill the cups. Jeff was on his shins, at the feet of Catherine who remained sitting on the sofa. She noticed this obvious dom/sub dynamic the same time as I did, and she gave me a wink. As Jeff finished pouring the third cup, Catherine extended her foot towards his mouth.

"Wanna lick my boot?"

"Uh, sure," Jeff replied. *No hesitation. Good man.* He handed her a glass of wine before repositioning his body so that he was more comfortable to begin licking. And Jeff did so with enthusiasm! His mouth went all over her leather, the wetness of his tongue adding a shine to her long black boot. Catherine casually took a sip from her cup as she observed his submissive worship, then looked to me with one raised eyebrow. I smiled and gave a shrug.

Jeff was becoming more interesting by the minute. Time for my tribute.

"For you, m´lady," I said with a bow, presenting the joint to her. Sitting down next to her, I offered her a flame from my disposable lighter. Catherine sucked it in, held it, and then leaned forward to blow out the smoke into my mouth. Our lips stayed together longer, and she allowed me a quick tease from the tip of her tongue before she leaned back.

"Slow down," she said to me with a wink. My cock was already a rock inside my jeans, and she knew it. She turned to Jeff, whose licking had progressed to the front of her ankle. "C´mere, my little slave. Let me say thank you."

Jeff joined us on the couch, and Catherine played the same game with him: took a big toke from the joint, held it, then exhaled the smoke into his mouth. He placed his hand tentatively on her bare shoulder, and her hand remained squeezing my thigh. Watching them kiss was turning me on.

Jeff´s cough broke the spell. He leaned forward, hacking up the smoke in tiny little bursts, before joining Catherine and me in laughter.

"Sorry," he said, picking up his cup, his cheeks the same color as the wine. "I don't really smoke pot…".

"No problem," Catherine purred, rubbing his back in circles. Her hand had moved higher up my inner thigh. "So. Which one of you kisses the best?"

Jeff looked literally tongue-tied, and when that image popped into my head, I laughed. He looked at me, then back at her.

"Why don't we let the Mistress of the house decide?" I

said, giving her and the universe a small toast with my mug.

"Mmmm, I like the sound of that," she said with a smile. She grabbed Jeff's jaw with one hand, and pulled him to her mouth.

Her kissing him felt like a tiny performance just for me, as well as something to satisfy Catherine's own pleasure. As their tongues danced inside their cheeks, her hand moved up my thigh and onto my stiff cock inside my pants. I finished my wine with a gulp, and put the mug down on the floor, hoping her hand wouldn't move away. Sitting back on the sofa and getting comfortable, I decided to chance it and touch her exposed thigh, right in the place between the bottom of her leather skirt and the top of her boot. I squeezed gently, and felt her hand squeeze me.

Catherine pulled away from Jeff, breathing deeply like a deep sea diver breaking the water's surface. His eyes remained on her heaving chest, her nipples barely hidden behind the top edge of her corset.

"It's okay, slave," she told him quietly, looking down at her large breasts. "Touch them, if you want."

Jeff began squeezing her breasts with his hands. Catherine arched her head back with a groan of delight, before turning towards me with heavy-lidded eyes. Her hand continued stroking the front of my pants as our mouths found each other's. Her tongue tasted warm and sweet, a perfect blend of wine, spit, smoke, and heat. I liked how she played with my bottom lip, giving it a little nibble when her tongue wasn't darting in and out of my mouth. My body squirmed on the sofa, aroused and activated through her mouth, and from her touch.

Then, suddenly, Catherine pulled away and stared hard into my eyes. She bit her bottom lip coyly, and it felt like something was about to shift. Jeff's hands and face were still worshiping her massive tits, which were spilling over the top of her corset now. He was sucking one of them like a hungry child. When his teeth came down a little too hard on one of her nipples, it made Catherine gasp–not with agony, though, but with pleasure. Holding onto my cock through my pants, I put my index finger into her open mouth. She began sucking it hard and slow, looking at me with a hunger that was surprisingly focused and direct for an almost-twenty- one-year-old.

Catherine gave my cock a little squeeze before pulling away. "Hey," she said, looking at her eager boys. "So, uh….you wanna try a threeway?"

Both of us nodded immediately, like two obedient little puppies. I could already feel my cock straining within my clothes. Would any guy answer no? Especially in the presence of someone as sexy as Catherine?

She smiled. The Mistress kissed Jeff first, helping him to take off his shirt promptly. I touched the breast closest to me, slowly beginning to play with the nipple between my thumb and index finger. Her bright pink areola contrasted beautifully with the ivory white of her skin and the obsidian of her revealing dominatrix costume. I pinched, and then I pulled. Catherine winced with plea-sure at every one of my little tweaks, and it was a turn-on watching her react to my fingers on your tit while her mouth devoured Jeff's. His hands cradled the sides of her face tenderly as her hands moved towards feeling his crotch. I looked there, too, and then watched as she opened her legs into a wide V.

I leaned forward to give her breast a sweet kiss of appreciation, and kept holding onto its tip with my hand as I knelt down between Catherine's legs. Beneath her skirt, she wore lacy black underwear, and I could smell her arousal through the fabric. She lifted her ass off of the couch briefly, so I could pull her thong down off of her thighs and down towards the ankles of her boots. Rather than go immediately towards her pussy right away, though, I instead began with the inside of her smooth white thighs. I squeezed them with my free hand, licked them with my mouth gently, just exploring and adoring, taking my time. Her hips responded with slow squirms, tiny tilts and arches, reveling in the sensations of our adoration. I knew she was yearning for me to go down on her quickly, to plunge my mouth onto her pussy, but I wanted to wait a little bit. Tease her. Make the Mistress beg for it.

Catherine pulled away from Jeff for a second, a confused look on her face. The top of his pants were unbuttoned and his cock was outside of his underwear, but he was only half-hard.

"Hey. Something wrong, baby?"

"No, uh, I just--". He turned red, and looked at me for a half second. "I'm just feeling a little self-conscious, I guess. I've never done anything like this before, and--".

"Maybe I can help," I said.

Moving over Catherine's lap I immediately swallowed Jeff's cock. And also immediately, I felt him swell inside of my mouth, filling me up. I began slowly bobbing my head up and down at an even pace, but didn't lose my attention on Catherine's perfect tit, whose nipple I began twisting harder as I got more and more excited. Giving head to a guy always turns me on. After a while, I removed my mouth from his dick, my hand continuing to stroke him. Jeff was good and stiff now, which made us all happy. I smiled.

"Jesus," Catherine exclaimed, her eyes wide. "I didn't know you were bi."

"Aren't we all," I asked wryly. I looked at both of them with a mischievous grin. "C'mon. I think we're all ready, now."

Jeff coughed, but had a giant grin on his face. Catherine had no problem letting out a loud laugh that started from her belly.

"Yeah, guys," she said. "Let's *fuck*."

"Yeah, baby!" I said, kissing her on the nose. "Not 'make love' or 'have sex'."

"*Fuck*," Jeff said, with emphasis.

"Right!" If I raised my palm just then, I think he would've given me a high-five.

"Sometimes, you just wanna *fuck*. Y'know?"

"Fuck yeah I do."

While Catherine began unfastening my pants, Jeff and I made out. He wasn't a bad kisser, as I recall, just kind of nervous. Maybe this was his first time having sex with *anyone*. Probably, this was his first time with a man and a woman at the same time. But, based on how he responded to my brief blowjob, he seemed game. I wonder who he fantasized more about, boys or girls?

Pulling away from Jeff's mouth, I looked down at my cock. Catherine was leaning forward and sucking me off, her mouth slurping and making low moans. Gently holding the back of her head, I slowly stood up. This way, she could sit more comfortably while I fucked her face.

Jeff quickly began taking off the rest of his clothes, and I took off my shirt, too. Catherine kept her corset and boots on, and I didn´t see any reason why that needed to change. She looked more and more sexy in that outfit.

I took out the handful of condoms from the pocket of my open jeans, letting them fall onto the table like rose petals. Catherine adjusted herself to recline onto the sofa, bunching her skirt up by her waist. She invited Jeff over to her first. Jeff didn't need to be told once, much less twice. He hurriedly tore off the wrapper of the condom with his teeth, and then quickly lay down on top of her. He began slowly pumping his cock inside of her, and I loved hearing them gasp the first time he slid inside of her. He was really focused on his task, like a teacher´s pet wanting that gold star.

I watched both of them fuck for a while–Jeff´s pale butt cheeks were clenching with each thrust, and Catherine´s eyes were rolling back into the back of her head. I took off the rest of my clothes, throwing them somewhere into the abyss of her dorm room. When I turned back, Catherine had placed her hands behind her knees, pulling them close to her chest, allowing Jeff to go deeper. He had one foot on the floor and a hand on the top of the sofa, like some kind of furniture yoga pose. In all seriousness, though, this nerd had a surprisingly good body. I smiled watching him, as well as Catherine´s delicious tits bouncing above her corset.

"Hey you," she said, waving me over. "Get that cock back here."

Placing my palms on the wall above the sofa, I bent my knees to guide my cock back into her warm open mouth. It was a little awkward, standing there with my knees bent and leaning forward, but I didn't mind. No, I didn't mind at all. Standing here, I was easily able to start playing with Jeff's chest while he fucked, experiment with giving his nipples a little twist. I could tell that what I was doing was making his dick grow thicker, making him pump Catherine a little harder. She whimpered as her mouth kept sliding up and down my cock. Between what all of us were doing to each other, I'd say we were all pretty goddamn satisfied.

Jeff reacheed his mouth towards mine for a kiss. Only this time, I teased him, only allowing our lips to have brief contact. I grabbed his hair to expose his neck, and then began kissing and licking him beneath his jaw. I liked feeling how his breathing changed with every move of my mouth as he continued to fuck Catherine between us.

This standing position I was in over the couch was getting uncomfortable, though; my muscles were getting sore from the effort, making me distracted from the fun we were beginning to have here. I pulled back. I wasn't in as good physical shape as these two undergrads, I guess. But Catherine seemed to want to change positions, too, as she gently pushed Jeff out of her so she could stand up. When she did, she wobbled for a second on her legs, which were still sheathed in her stiletto heeled boots. I quickly grabbed her by the waist so that she wouldn't fall, and the three of us laughed for a moment.

Catherine began kissing me, nice and slow. Her tongue was thick and hungry, and when she pulled back from me for a second, I saw that Jeff had stood up, too. He stood right behind her, and began slobbering the tops of her shoulders with his mouth. His hands holding her corset on either side of her ribs brought my attention back to her neck, her collarbones, her gorgeous fucking tits. Catherine lifted her arms above her head, touching Jeff's sweaty hair as he nuzzled behind her. She looked absolutely gorgeous.

"Jesus. You look like a goddess," I said.

"Really?" she panted, raising an eyebrow.

"Yeah," I said, twisting both of her nipples hard. "A fucking *sex* goddess."

"Or maybe," she whimpered, "just a fucking *slut*."

"What's the difference?"

Still standing, Catherine bent forward at her hips, her mouth swallowing me all the way down in one gulp. Her bare ass now wiggled back towards Jeff, inviting him in. This girl even placed a hand on one of her cheeks, so he could slide himself back inside of her pussy more easily, without breaking the rhythm of her head bouncing up and down on my cock. *Slut. Goddess.* Finally inside, Jeff gripped her hips, while I moved her beautiful long hair out of the way, clutching it like a bouquet. The three of us soon found a tempo together, nice and slow, each of us fucking at the altar of this goddess.

Damn, Catherine! What an amazing fucking slut you are. Slut-goddess. Perfect little fuck-bitch. It felt so goddamn good.

Jeff seemed to be having a hard time keeping it up, though. Maybe because

of us all being in this standing? I definitely wasn't having that problem, especially in this raunchy spit-roast position. Why was his cock getting soft? I couldn't tell. Quickly, though, Catherine sensed something was off too, and instructed us to change things up again. She was definitely running the show here. She was our Mistress, and our Goddess, at least for tonight.

"Here, lie back, baby," she told Jeff, giving him a little push. He sat down onto the sofa, while she moved the table aside. Catherine knelt down on the hardwood floor in front of him, and pulled the condom off of his half-limp dick. She hacked up some good spit onto the head of it, and began to rapidly stroking him with her hand.

"It's okay, baby," she whispered to him. "Oh yeah. Yes, make it hard for me, baby. I need it. That's it. Oh yeah, I fucking need it."

Still kneeling, Catherine then arched her lower back to reach around and unfasten her leather skirt, which fell onto the hardwood floor with a heavy thump. She turned over her shoulder to look at me below the waist.

"*You* seem ready to go," she said. It was less of a question, and more of an observation. My cock felt as hard as one the wooden legs of the table next to her. I knelt down behind her and slapped her bare ass. Hard. My palm left a tiny red stain on the surface of her skin.

"Ow, fuck yeah," Catherine grunted. "That's what I'm talking about."

When I didn´t spank her again, she wiggled her ass in my face. This girl clearly wanted more.

"C´mon, Daddy," she whined, looking over my shoulder, biting her lower lip. "I've been a really *bad* girl."

She kept jerking Jeff off, and I began spanking her ass. Each time, her buttock would get a little pink, and each time, my cock would grow a little more stiff, too. Catherine swallowed Jeff, who grabbed her hair so that none of it would get into her mouth as she sucked. I watched her back and neck muscles snake up and down for a moment while she worked him, spanking her gorgeous ass a few more times while I got a condom on. Once it was on, I bent forward to lick her pussy. She tasted sweet and warm, and her ass smelled earthy.

"Oh Jesus," she yelped, breaking away from Jeff's cock. "I'm close. I'm close! Just fucking put that fucking dick inside of me!"

Who can refuse a goddess? Kneeling behind her, I slowly slid my cock inside of her effortlessly. Catherine's pussy felt tight, so I tried to go slow with my thrusts at first, *I swear*. But this slut-goddess was just too goddamn hot, and I was just too fucking turned on. *Fuck it.* Holding onto the sides of her hips, I began riding her hard, my hips pounding her much more than Jeff did earlier. She seemed like it, although I couldn't tell at first because his dick was still stuffed deep inside her mouth. Jeff had his hands on the back of her head, pushing her down onto him further, and it sounded like she was starting to gag. The sounds, the intense animal-struggle of it all, just made me fuck her harder. Jeff was watching me fuck her, and I wondered what it would be like to fuck his tight little ass. My eyes rolled into the back of my head with the image.

Opening them again, I looked down at Catherine's gorgeous and perfect slut body. A sheen of sweat covered her upper back, above the corset. I slapped her ass again. Her moans got lower, more guttural.

"That's it, baby. Take it."

Jeff continued to look at me from heavy-lidded eyes as I fucked the goddess from behind. What was turning him on more: getting sucked off by this slut, or watching me fuck her from behind? Did he even know the answer to that question? I met his stare, then looked down at her waist. I liked how her cheeks quivered with each thrust of my pounding hips, the sound of our sweaty flesh slapping up against one another.

Catherine pulled her head off of Jeff then. Her breathing was loud, percussive, and in sync with the rhythm of my thrusts. She kept jerking him off with her hand, and I pulled on one of her shoulders to help keep her lifted up. I wanted to watch her face as it shifted into a kind of desperate ecstasy. I loved listening to her voice, rising in pitch and volume as she abandoned herself even more into the sex. We were seeing our real faces, now. Witnessing the most private and intimate expressions we had.

"Oh shit, I'm gonna come," Jeff shouted. His hips were lifting off of the top of the sofa, trying to return to Catherine, to be surrounded by her wet warmth.

She engulfed his cock into her mouth again, and after his whine through gritted teeth, I could hear her swallowing. *Oh, good girl,* I thought. I slowed down my rhythm so she could get it all down, as well as allow us all to catch our breath for a second. My knees were a little sore from being on the hardwood floor, and I wondered if hers were hurting too. Somehow, though, this pain didn't really take away from the excitement of what we were doing. The pain and the pleasure had all mixed in together, becoming one thing.

Catherine pulled up from Jeff, and wiped off her mouth with the back of her wrist. She then pushed him away from her, and placed both palms onto the floor. She pushed her ass back against me in a slow, steady rhythm.

"Take a little break," she told him, then looked over her shoulder at me. "I wanna focus...on *this*...right here."

"Oh yeah, baby," I grunted. "That's it, fuck me back."

I watched Catherine bounce her hips back and up against me, then leaned

forward to grab some of her long brown hair. I wrapped it a couple of times around my hand, then pulled it back like the reins on a horse. She let out a grunt of approval, and so I yanked her hair back again, making her arch her back more. With my other hand, I began slapping her ass again. I told Catherine to ride it, to go faster. And she did. This slut-goddess was much stronger than I thought. She kept pushing her ass back against me, and I just kept riding her.

"Jesus *fuck*," she yelled, after a while. "You gonna fuckin' come yet?"

"Unh-unh," I said. "Not yet, bitch." I pulled her hair back even more. Her back was really arched now, as much as it could be while still wearing her corset. I used every muscle I could to get inside of her, to get more of me into Catherine's perfect wet pussy.

She turned back to look at me, my hand still clutching her hair. She looked aroused, but her face also showed a tinge of fear. Was she just used to boys like Jeff here, who came in five minutes? Was it because she was scared about how much she was liking this rough stuff? Maybe she had never had sex with two people at once, either. Maybe she wasn't used to being with an older guy. I leaned forward, placing my mouth close to her ear.

"Come on, Catherine, ride me," I said, before straightening back up. "You can take it. That's what you came here for, right?"

25

I let go of her hair. We pulled and pushed up against one another, a wrestling dance of desire and desperation. Catherine really wanted to make me come, and I just wouldn't. Even with all of the booze I´d had so far tonight, I concentrated on holding it in. I wanted to see how many times I could make this slut come first. She was dressed as a goddess tonight, and deserved to get really really laid.

I noticed Jeff, who was looking at us. He liked what he saw, but I felt like we were making him feel a little left out. I stopped and nodded towards him.

"Okay, your turn," I said. I pulled out of Catherine, and she seemed to appreciate the break. She had been on her knees for a while now, and I bet they were more sore than mine were. I motioned Jeff off the couch so I could sit down, and told him to kneel on the floor in front of me.

"You ever suck a man´s dick before, Jeff?" I asked.

He looked to Catherine first, and then back to me. He shook his head.

"You´ll figure it out," Catherine said. She laughed as she leaned forward to kiss me, then got some revenge by twisting my nipples. She did it hard, but I didn't mind. My cock grew even stiffer, and it felt great to get that condom ripped off so Jeff´s warm mouth could suck it. He was tentative and careful, but if I'm honest, his inexperience was also part of the turn on. After a while, Catherine sat down next to me, watching him suck me. Her hand made little circles in-between her legs.

"What the fuck will make you *come*," she asked. "Jesus fucking *Christ*."

I laughed. "Never considered that a *problem* before."

"No, but seriously," she said. "I feel like he and I have

gotten what we wanted. I mean, it's your turn. Isn't there anything we can do?"

I smiled at the return of her Marilyn impersonation, and then whispered into her ear. She looked at me, with an inscrutable expression on her face. She moistened her lips with the tip of her pink tongue, and then said quietly, "I've never done that before."

"I have. Once," I said. "You want to try it?"

She looked at Jeff, and then back at me. She nodded. "But go *slow*."

"Of course," I said, and kissed her tenderly on the mouth. "I think you'll like it. And if not, just tell me, and I 'll stop."

I pulled Jeff's head away from my cock, and told him to lie down on the floor, on his back. I tossed him a fresh condom, and placed a couple of pillows on either side of him while he was putting it on. I looked at Catherine, who handed me a tiny bottle of lube.

"You sure you wanna do this?"

She nodded. "Just go slow, okay?"

I kissed her mouth, then gave her ass a gentle thwack. She gave my face a tiny slap, then straddled on top of Jeff. Her knees and shins were cushioned from the hardwood floor this time, as I wanted the goddess to be as comfortable as possible. Catherine slowly lowered her dripping wet pussy over his stiff cock, using her hand to guide it in, until he was all the way in. She began rocking her hips, slow and steady, taking her time. She braced herself with her hands on the floor on either side of his head. Her corset had slipped down some, her breasts totally free above Jeff's face. I was surprised that it was still on her, at this point.

27

Dress to get laid.

"Twist her nipples, Jeff," I directed. "Keep this slut nice and wet."

I put on the last condom, getting turned on watching them fuck like this. Catherine's hips were really working his dick, and I could tell that she was purposefully teasing him by rocking into him slow and deep. The cheeks of her pale ass were still splotched pinkish-red from the earlier spankings, and I knew they must still be sensitive. I carefully knelt down behind the two of them, and placed my palm on her lower back, slick with sweat.

"Arch your ass up, babe," I instructed her. "High as you can, but don't let Jeff's cock slip out. Okay?"

"Okay," she panted, looking at me. She had that same expression on her face as before. This wasn't fear; this was *thrill,* the desire for danger, like someone going onto a rollercoaster for the first time. I told her to hold still, and aimed the tip of my lubed up cock in between her beautiful cheeks. I placed one hand onto her breast, whose nipple was hard like a tiny stone, and played with it. Below me, I saw her tight little asshole breathe open. Using one hand on the hilt of my cock, I slowly moved into her.

"Unh," she said. "Unnnnnhhhhhhhh!...."

"That's it, Catherine," I said, holding her back by the shoulder. "You can do it, baby."

"Oh fuck," Jeff said below us. "Oh fuck!"

"Let me know when you're gonna come, buddy," I said.

At first, I thought Catherine might be too tight, that our attempt at a double-penetration threesome wasn't going to happen tonight. But then I felt the head of my cock plug inside her, and we all moaned with primal pleasure. The ring of her anus was constricting and releasing around my cock, and Catherine´s breathing suddenly got faster. I kept soothing her with my words, barely moving my hips forward, giving her time to adjust to it. I remembered the first time I had gotten fucked up the ass, and knew that it felt uncomfortable at first, as well as a little weird. But Catherine was already starting to move her hips back up against me, trying to get more of me inside of her. She was getting into this more quickly than I thought, or could have hoped for. Definitely into anal sex far more readily that I was, for my first time.

Such a good girl. Such a sexy fucking slut-goddess.

"Oh! OH!" she shouted. Catherine´s nails dug into Jeff ´s chest below. She turned her head towards me, but her eyes were squeezed tight. "Go slow, go slow," she whispered. "This is a first!"

"I know, baby," I said. I twisted her nipple again, and her ass bucked back towards me almost immediately. Gently but firmly, I was getting more of my cock inside her tight little asshole. Catherine took a deep inhale of breath.

"Oh my fucking GOD," she yelled. "Two dicks! One in my ass, one inside my pussy? Oh my *fucking* CHRIST!"

And then, just like that, the Mistress was back in charge again. Catherine established our rhythm, rocking her hips–back up against me, and down against Jeff. *Double-fucked*. Jeff lifted his head off of the floor, craning his neck so he could suck on the nipple of one of her dangling breasts. I placed my hands on the top of her shoulders, holding her to keep her back arched.

"Jesus *fuck*!" she howled."That feels so *fucking* good."

"You´re so good, baby," I quietly encouraged her. "Now

29

run to it. You hear me? Keep breathing. Run to it. Come on."

Catherine began speaking in a way I'd never heard from her before. She sounded possessed, her whimpers blending pleasure with ache, her discomfort turning into a kind of rage. She began yelling at Jeff to suck her tits. Then commanded me to slap her ass until it was red. All the while, she kept moving nonstop, her beautiful hips pumping harder into us. The words coming out of her mouth just got more and more nasty.

"Come on," she said, looking at me directly in the eyes this time. "*Come on*! Fuck that ass. That's it: *fuck it.* Fuck it *hard.* Make it *come.* I'm gonna make you *come.* Oh *fuck....*"

Her words became like a chant, or the verses of a profane spell. I felt my control slipping, as the moment pulled me irrevocably closer to the edge, the one I knew I would not be able to resist much longer. Holding onto her shoulders, I began moving my body more. I was pumping her ass harder, going deeper than I ever thought I could. I felt like every part of my body was straining, but Catherine yelled at me to not stop, not stop. I couldn't believe this was her first time doing anal, much less doing it with another guy inside her too. Catherine was totally into it. Wild, a timeless moment that I wish could last forever. She could tell from my hips that something had changed inside me. She could tell that this time, I was close.

"You coming, baby?"

"Unh," I grunted. "UNH!"

"You gonna *come*?" she asked again, louder. "I want you to COME!"

"Unh!"

"That's right," Jeff said beneath her. "Fuck that tight little ass!"

"Come for me, fucker," she said, her mouth snarling. "Give it to me. Yeah? Come. Come! You gonna come? Huh?

"Yeah," I said. I tightened the muscles in my lower belly as much as I could, but it was no good. "Ohhhh, fuck," I yelled, "I'm gonna blow!"

I pulled out just in time. I didn't want to take the chance of the condom breaking. I fell back onto the floor. The condom held, my ejaculate filling it like water inside a balloon.

Catherine looked at me with a smile, her face radiant. She then turned her focus entirely to Jeff's straining body beneath her. The goddess was more powerful than us, more powerful than maybe she even realized. She began rocking her hips forward and back with even more effort.

"Your turn, motherfucker," she said with an evil grin, looking down at him. "Do it. Come on! Give it to me!"

Almost immediately, Jeff arched his back up, his hands grabbing both of her ass cheeks as he pushed up off the floor as high as he could. His hips spasmed, and he let out a sound that sounded like his skin had been lit on fire.

For a while, the three of us just lay there, breathing and moaning, the hardwood floor still warm from our bodies and from our sweat. Catherine between us, her two supplicants having seen the face of the goddess, and been forever transformed. I remember the sound of our collective breathing, and how I wished we could have just stayed like that, on Catherine's floor, forever. I felt like we had all just run up a mountain, done something hard that none of us thought we could do. But now that we had, we fell quiet, suddenly at peace.

And then I passed out. Maybe I had some major spiritual experience? Maybe I had just gotten exhausted from all of the crazy fucking and the booze? I don't know. The two tend to feel the same a lot of the time.

WHEN I CAME TO, it was still dark. It must have been at some point later that same night. I looked around, and found myself alone. The floor had grown cold. Where was Jeff? Where was the goddess? I slowly stood up, the muscles of my thighs and lower back feeling sore, but good. I found my clothes in a pile, on top of a chair. Except for the half-empty wine bottle, I didn't see any trace of Jeff. The wrappers and used condoms had all been thrown away.

I put on my underwear and jeans, and walked carefully through the dark. I went into the room Catherine had gone to earlier, when she handed me the lube, as I guessed it was her bedroom. I saw her curled up in her bed, facing the wall. No Jeff. Instead of going back to my room, I decided to stay here tonight. I climbed in, spooning behind her. I fell asleep to the sound of her breathing, and the memories of our time together.

I STUMBLED AWAKE AGAIN SOMETIME before dawn. The sky was purple now, instead of black. When I opened my eyes, Catherine was now facing me. She was already awake, and had an expression on her face I didn't recognize. I smiled, and tried nestling closer to her, thinking maybe we could cuddle. She stayed as still as the ground beneath our feet.

"You should go," she said, matter-of-factly.

"Oh. Sure. Totally," I said.

Before I finished getting dressed in the other room, Catherine had gone into the bathroom. I heard the faint sound of a shower running. I left feeling like a thief who has no idea what he stole.

Outside, I looked down towards the end of the Lawn, towards the end of the world. I figured I'd skip breakfast, maybe just head back to Franklin myself and go back to sleep. I saw a familiar figure crossing the grass and heading towards me. Because, I guess, on the Walk of Shame, it's Murphy's Law that you run into someone. But was I ashamed? I felt like a bunch of things were running through me, all at the same time. The figure got close to me, and I gave her a nod.

"Hail Satan," Emilee said.

"Hail," I said, running my hand through my hair. It felt sticky.

"Well. You look like shit," she laughed.

"Fuck you very much," I said. "You have a cigarette?"

She took two out of her pack. After she lit them both, she gave me one. We stood there smoking, watching the sky turn from purple to gold.

"Working?" I asked.

"Yeah," she said, waving her hand a couple of times in a vain attempt to keep her smoke from getting into my face. "I have to finish this project this weekend, so I've basically been living in my studio VAPA."

"Getting some stuff done?"

Emilee blushed, which is not something you see very often on her. "I....let's just say that I had a....*significant breakthrough* last night."

"Do tell," I teased. "Did you partake in the Dress to Get Laid party?"

"Are you serious," she snorted.

"That's right, you *live* there," I said, nodding in sympathy. "So....sounds like you stayed....*elsewhere*."

She shrugged. "It was a good night. You?"

Behind my cigarette, I didn't even try to hide my big grin. Emilee punched my arm.

"You fucker," she said, laughing. "Tell me."

"Let me shower first," I said, "and then we swap stories of our nocturnal adventures over pancakes."

"You're on."

"Love you, Em," I said.

EVERYTHING IS A DRAWING

"Prove me wrong," Emilee said. "I dare you."

She was looking up from the drafting table where she was working on a new piece. That´s right: Saturday night, and she was *here*, trying to make some art, instead of going to that stupid fucking Dress to Get Laid party. Which was probably just as well, she decided, as those stupid fucks from Canfield, the granola-crunchy ones who refused to shower, were all probably there, anyway.

Here was the studio Emilee shared with CJ, at the Visual and Performing Arts building, way over on the opposite side of campus. True, there were a few other worker bees in the cavernous building tonight, each doing their little art-thing, making their projects. The only one she knew was Troy, next door. He was preparing to weld something, Emilee surmised, as she could see him through the open door of her studio, making trips back and forth through the hallway, lugging a bundle of scrap metal every other time. Like her own little movie. The fact that Emilee found this "movie" more engaging than her artwork was depressing.

This all happened years ago, back in college. Back when Emileee still had long hair. And only three tattoos.

Instead of dressing up to get laid, or at least getting drunk and high at a party this Saturday night, Emilee was working on a series of drawings for her class "100 Drawings". She was working from scratch, having discarded her earlier set the night before. *Discarded* being a euphemism for *destroyed in a drunken rage by setting them on fire.* Not really that uncommon, and not necessarily even that big of a deal, within the artistic process. Sometimes, you have to go through a hundred pieces of shit to find one nugget of gold, she told herself. However, what really really sucked about this particular situation, though, was the timing and the context. Emilee had to present a hundred drawings on Monday. She needed to get those crits and check those boxes, show her teacher and this goddamn College that yes indeed, she *had* been working on her art all semester long. Yessireebob.

Which she *had*, Emilee thought; any *real* visual artist would know and understand. Just...not always in a strictly *visible* sense. Or even in a...*consistent* or *cognizant* manner. Everything she did, thought, or felt part of the process was part of the process...right? Unfortunately, at this stage of Emilee´s creative development, this was still *college*, where things had to be shown to specific people on specific days and times, shit like that. As if everyone was artistic in the same way, or that creativity followed a fourteen-week semester schedule. How did all of the other students here do it?

Basically, this weekend, Emilee was cramming, trying

to get enough drawings together that she could share without vomiting. She needed to buckle down and jump through these hoops, get one step closer to graduating from this place. She imagined herself with her arms extended to her sides, like a bird or a kite, the Four Winds floating her away from here. She smiled fondly at the image, and considered putting that down on paper.

No crits meant no grade. And no grade meant no graduation.

C'mon, Em, she told herself. She put down her pencil, and slapped her cheeks to upload some fresh energy into her brain. *You can do this, you can do this.*

Her friends on and off-campus ribbed her for stressing out about any of it. They said that her panic attacks and bouts of insomnia were all unfounded, assuring her that this school was basically *impossible to fail* out of. On that point, Emilee was technically in agreement, and didn't think they were gaslighting her or just blowing smoke up her ass. What really scared her, though, was slipping into some kind of five- (or six-) year plan here, as she saw a number of her peers doing. Emilee refused to fall into that category. Fuck that. Maybe if you have a trust fund you can wander around this spooky corner of New England for an extra year or two and take more and more classes where you "learn by doing". That wasn't Emilee's style. She wanted to be done with school. She wanted to graduate and start life. Get a crappy over-priced apartment somewhere in Brooklyn, work at a bar or something. Emilee just wanted to make art, do better drugs than anything she could find here in Vermont, have the money to cover her body in more tattoos, and make out with lots of hot chicks.

Basically, live the dream.

But to get from here to there, she needed to jump through a few more hoops.

"Okay. What about ballet, then?" CJ asked. "Dance is three-dimensional. Drawings are only 2-D."

Emilee smiled at the challenge arising from the other side of the studio. She remained hunched over her own paper, though, underscoring her answer with long strokes of her pen. "Uh, hello, CJ? Ever heard of *line*? Like, the line in the *body*? Lines in *space*? Those are part of the foundational vocabularies of dance. And a line, of course, is also a drawing. So, as I said earlier, and has already been well-established: everything is a drawing."

"Bitch."

"Just stop trying to fight it," Emilee chuckled, "it'll be easier."

CJ was Emilee's studio-mate, a transplant originally from Colorado, kneeling before a towering sculpture on the other side of their shared space, intent on the work at hand. Wearing a red and white flannel shirt over a black tank-top, CJ had her sleeves rolled up, showing off intricate tattoos that rippled across her wiry forearms everytime she handled something. Her glasses looked like she swiped them off of Buddy Holly, but her crew cut made her ready to start basic training for some military death-squad. Even without her wearing the scuffed pair of Doc Martens, CJ was all butch.

Emilee looked up, and saw Troy passing the doorway again. Empty handed this time. *How many more trips is he going to make,* she mused. She wondered what he was building next door. She wondered if *he* was crystal clear about what he was building next door, actually, based on what she could remember how he described his project in class. Something about an...outdoor sound structure? Exploring kinetic form, whatever the hell that means? Something like that. She remembered what he told the class last week, when everyone asked to give a brief update on their progress. *Yeah,* he'd mumbled, his blonde surfer-dude hair falling in front of his eyes. *I'm exploring the, like,* kinesthesia *in the sound space, y'know? Oh, and like....*BODIES. *Yeah. Investigating the structural framework of it all, the whole auditorial....*

Emilee shook her head, trying to turn the recollection back down to mute. Thinking about Troy, and how everything he said was interpreted as genius always pissed her off, and she hoped a headache wasn't coming on. *Fucker will probably get an A,* she thought to herself. She needed to focus on her own work.

She looked at the page she had been drawing some lines on, and then crumpled it with a groan. She tossed it to the wastebasket, but it was already full with her other failures. Emilee got out a fresh page, and wondered if switching from ink to charcoal would help.

"All right," CJ chirped. "How about *people*? Say, a *politician*? What about President Bush?"

"You ever met Dubya in real life?" Emilee snorted. "No. Neither have I. Neither has anyone we know."

"Yeah, so...?"

"So," Emilee continued, lengthening out the vowel, "he's just a picture on the fuckin'*tee-vee*. And a picture is....?"

"A drawing. Okay, sure. You got me."

"Very good, grasshopper."

CJ turned her attention back to her mixed-media sculpture, shifting around its base to peer at it critically from different angles. Over the semester, Emilee had noticed her adding objects to it regularly, creating a kind of layered chronicle of her thought-process during its creation. Tonight, silverware swiped from the dining hall seemed to be the thing. After gluing a final fork onto part of the tower, CJ stood up, her knees cracking audibly. Emilee watched her cross to the small sink next to the small refrigerator in the corner to wash her hands, and wondered what CJ wore beneath those worn-out jeans.

"Wanna beer?" she asked.

"Nah," Emilee said, looking back down to her paper. "Maybe later." She drew some lines, but all of them were curved, and bore a striking resemblance to CJ´s ass. "Wish I had some fucking pot, though," she added.

"Probably some at the Dress to Get Laid party."

Emilee looked up, her gaze sharper than a penknife. CJ nearly choked on her beer, and put up a palm.

"What? I'm just sayin´."

"What *exactly* are you saying?" Emilee leaned back on her stool, her arms forming an X across her chest.

"Nothing, Em. *Jesus*! I´m just saying that--that there's probably some good drugs there."

Emilee stood up, though once she was back on her feet, she seemed to lack any kind of direction. "Ha! *Good*? Yeah, right. And if there are, there´s probably a half dozen *dudes* that I´d have to make stupid small talk with, just to get it. They'd probably make me offer them all a blowjob, just to get a hit. And tonight? I am just... not. In. the. MOOD."

"Whoa. Em. What is *up*?"

Em stood in the opposite corner, her back to the studio and to CJ.

Unseen, Troy stopped his sortie for a second glance inside their studio, seeing what the two chicks from class were up to. Immediately sensing that the vibe in there was a little heavy, he shrugged his shoulders and before continuing his surfer shuffle back to his truck for the last armful of scrap.

"You wanna talk?"

When Emilee spun around, black mascara trailed down her cheeks in two rivulets. "What is there to talk about? I'm just---stressing the fuck out, okay?"

"About...your project due Monday?"

"Sure. Yeah, *that*. But also....I don't know. *Everything!*" Fresh tears leaked

from her eyes, but instead of providing relief, crying only seemed to fill Emilee with greater frustration. She typically didn't like showing that kind of vulnerability in public. "Tonight I just...feel like a fucking *dork*," she continued. "I mean, it's like all I fucking *do* is just spend my nights working on these *fucking drawings*. Everyone else is out partying and getting high or getting laid."

"Hey," CJ said quietly. "I'm not at that party. Don't put me with those fuckers. I'm here. With you."

Emilee wiped the snot away from her nose with her wrist, and then tried to interpret the purpose behind CJ's comment. "I know. Sorry. I'm just...."

"Being a whiny bitch?"

Emilee laughed, breaking the tension that was beginning to box her in. CJ was good at that. Her humor was like a blowtorch, burning a cut through the drama.

"So basically," she continued matter-of-factly, "you're just having a little pity-party over there?"

"Fuck you," Emilee said. She used the bottom edge of her shirt to wipe away the last of her make-up.

CJ shifted her weight onto one leg, and placed her hands on her strong hips, just above her black leather belt. "You said, everything is a drawing, right?"

Emilee nodded. "Yep. I'm famous for that theory."

CJ untucked her flannel shirt, and began unbuttoning it. "So. Draw *me*."

Emilee blinked, swallowed. All of her bodily functions suddenly sounded loud in the studio.

"And if you tell anyone--and I mean *anyone*--that I let you use me as a model? I will totally kick your ass."

"Understood."

Emilee crossed back to her drafting table. At her stool, she picked up a fresh stack of paper, and put their blank pages in front of her. Instead of picking up the pen, though, she grabbed a stick of charcoal: she wanted the possibility of broader brush strokes, lines which could capture the energy of the moment. More motion and feeling, impulse; less thinking.

Looking up, CJ was already taking off her second boot. She had placed her clothes, folded, into a neat little square on top of a paint can. Now, she wore only her black tank top and a pair of white boxers. Besides the tattoos on her forearms, Emilee noticed another, smaller design just over CJ's heart, halfway hidden beneath the strap of her top. Her limbs were muscular, her skin pale, her legs unshaven. Little horizontal scars ran on the top of her thighs, near her groin. Emilee felt they were the most private part of her, far more than any other naked body she had ever seen.

"What do you want me to do?" she asked.

Emilee dropped into artist mode. At least, she did her best to, as she could feel her nipples growing hard beneath her faded Type O Negative t-shirt. "Uh, go over there," she said, "next to that wall."

"Okay. Now what?"

Emilee began making broad strokes with the charcoal. Something was beginning to emerge from the paper. She could almost see it, like a fish swimming beneath the surface. This time, she wasn't going to let it go. She was going to catch that motherfucker. "Just--do anything you want," she said, her hand moving faster and faster. "I'm just--going to try and get some of these ideas down...This is good, CJ."

It really was. Emilee hadn't done any art with a model in...she couldn't remember how long. She felt inspired, renewed. She knew that the electricity tingling through her body was due in large part to having one of the most private people on campus standing half-naked in front of her. Or maybe it was just adrenalin, the crunch of needing to get a shit-ton of work completed within the next 36 hours? Or maybe, if she were honest with herself, it was because Emilee had had a secret crush on CJ, but never had the guts to tell her. And now here she was. Here *they* were.

CJ kept her Buddy Holly glasses on. Emilee moved her arm faster and faster, the energetic images forming on her cascading pages more and more. Each time she looked at her model, she just stood there simply and unafraid. Way more courageous than Emilee ever felt. Emilee tried to hold CJ's stare, but she couldn't match it, choosing instead to return to the table. CJ's eyes were too calm, too penetrating. Even though she was the one barely wearing any clothes, Emilee felt like she was the one that was being exposed.

A dozen pages fell to the floor, then two dozen–each one filled with impulsive shapes and fragmented lines. The preciousness and caution of her earlier attempts were replaced with a new vision, seeds that Emilee could develop later into a good set. She wasn't thinking; she was feeling, going with the flow. Her chattering mind had quieted down, like the volume on a boom box being turned down. Emilee became the paper and the charcoal. And CJ.

In the doorway, Troy paused, his hands wrapped around a bundle of disorganized metal, and peered in. Emilee noticed him, but didn't give a fuck. She'd caught hold of her flow again, something that she hadn't felt in a long time, and wasn't about to let it go.

"Come here," CJ commanded. "Bring the charcoal."

Confused, Emilee silently opened and closed her mouth, like a fish pulled out of the depths and laying on the floor of a boat. Before she could find her voice, CJ shouted: "We know you're there, Troy!" The model turned to the doorway, then back to Emilee, then back to Troy. She then took off her black tank top.

"If you're going to stand there and watch, then that's it: *watch only.* Got it?" She turned back to Emilee. "And close the door behind you," CJ added.

Troy dropped the pile of metal onto the floor, making a loud clang outside the studio. Their echoing cacophony muted once he closed the door behind him. Troy slid down so that he sat with his back to it, looking at the two women like a kid about to watch a movie.

CJ just breathed for a moment, standing, coming to a

decision. The areola of her breasts were light pink and large, and they stared at Emilee with an intensity equal to her new model's gaze. And tonight, the artist stared back, breathing it all in. She savored the details of CJ's body, even noticed some goosebumps beginning to ripple across the surface of her bare skin.

When CJ reached for her glasses, Emilee extended her hand. "No," she said. "Keep those on. They look good on you."

"Thanks," she blushed.

Usually so strong and solid, CJ now seemed awkward, even shy. The model shifted her weight back and forth between her feet, as if uncertain where to go or what to do. Emilee stepped away from her drafting table, and walked right up to CJ's nearly-naked body. She could almost smell the anticipation between them, mixed in with the charcoal.

"Draw me," CJ whispered.

Lifting her hand, Emilee placed the tip of the charcoal on CJ's skin. She began with her collarbones, that small curve where the two meet the sternum. Tiny little bones, connecting the entire shoulder-girdle. Fragile and strong, at the same time. Slowly, she drew a black vertical line down between CJ's breasts, and saw the tiny ridges of her goosebumps rising to meet the charcoal's blunt tip. The breathing of the two women, of the artist and model, began to slow down, synchronizing into one pulse as they plunged into their new world deeper.

CJ smiled. Emilee leaned forward and kissed her on the lips.

She had come out as lesbian before leaving her child-hood home in Maine and coming to Vermont for college, but Emilee´s experiences with other women up to this point were still limited to what she could count on a single hand. And of those, if truth be told, all had occurred while at least one of them was wasted on drugs or alcohol. CJ was the first woman Emilee had kissed while stone cold sober. And she liked it. She could taste and feel every part of it, and it bloomed a sweet nostalgia within her belly. This was how anyone's first time should be. Sweet, soft, tender. She used to think it was a cliché, but Emilee now knew how accurate the expression "got weak in the knees" was. Really hit the bullseye, there.

The two gently explored each other's mouths, discovering a mutual hunger that felt new between them. CJ was the first to withdraw slowly from the kiss. Taking the charcoal out of Emilee´s hand, she drew a zig-zagging line down the outside of Em´s face, like half of a death-mask.

"There," CJ said. "Now *you* are a drawing."

"Enough theory," she smiled.

Emilee wrapped her hands around CJ´s neck, and kissed her mouth again. The first kiss was tentative and shy; this one roamed with its appetite. She liked feeling CJ´s strong arms pull her slender body closer, almost as much as her round breasts pressing against her own smaller ones. Emilee made her hands into loving claws and scratched CJ's naked back. The model made a pleasing little squeal, so the artist scratched again.

After a moment, CJ turned around, her back pressed against Emilee. She fixed her intense gaze on Troy, who remained seated on the floor, enthralled. If there was a bowl of popcorn, he´d be eating it.

"You like this?"

Troy nodded his head in response to her question. He

wasn't a man-child: with that dopey smile of his, he looked more like a puppy.

"It's not for you," CJ said.

She raised her arms above her head, reaching back to touch Emilee's. CJ squirmed with delight when a necklace of kisses began to encircle her neck and tops of her shoulders. She tried using the charcoal to draw whatever part of Emilee she could find, but soon let it drop to the floor with a faint crack. She wanted both of her hands available for whatever happened next. Emilee lightly grazed the side of the model's bare ribs, before sliding around to cup her breasts with adoring squeezes. Both of them felt wet between their legs, and a rush of energy was causing CJ to step forward now. She pivoted to face Emilee, and caught her breath. She then spread her muscular hairy legs into a wide V.

"Have you ever seen another woman's cunt?"

Emilee shook her head.

"Wanna see mine?"

Emilee nodded. She had only had sex with two other women here at the College, so far. Both times, they were drunk, and both times, in the dark. But now, tonight, Emilee was standing here in a brightly lit art studio, with CJ offering to show her holiest of holies. And dumbass Troy sat watching all of it.

And yet, somehow, this didn't seem all that strange. It felt like Emilee was making progress in her life, actually.

Ah, college....

With her back to the boy and the door he came in through, CJ bent forward slightly to slide her boxers off. She winced slightly as she sat down, feeling the floor's cool temperature on her bare ass. Using her fingers, she spread open her lips. Emilee got close to the floor too, crawling forward to see her up close. She noticed the scars again, on the inside of her thighs, and estimated that there were at least twenty on either side. She got close enough to smell CJ, an arousing and pungent scent like sweet vinegar. Her nose, only one or two inches from CJ's hairy pussy, was close to so many nerve endings, from the power that moved the world. The entrance to the mystery of life.

"Kiss it," CJ said.

Emilee looked past CJ's shoulder and caught Troy craning his own neck, trying to see what was unfolding between the two women. She dove in. She hoped that her relative lack of experience wouldn't make any sort of negative impact on CJ. But as she licked and kissed her, Emilee asked herself: had she ever seen this tough, confident-seeming woman with anyone else? Sure, she *appeared* to be the most "out" woman on campus, but CJ held the details of her personal life close to the chest. Who knows? Maybe this was the first time for both of them.

Resting her forearms on the cold floor, Emilee cradled CJ's hips, using her lips and tongue more intently. She began to suck on CJ's lips, and nibble. Like kissing, it was all about taste and exploration. And paying attention.

Clearly, CJ enjoyed Emilee's roving mouth. She cradled the back of the artist's head and held her close. Her hips began to gently rock against Emilee's mouth and face, getting into it. She moaned, her sound muffled, while CJ's voice echoed off of the studio's walls.

"Holy *shit!*" she shouted. "Fuck….*YEAH*!......damn….".

Through her mouth, Emilee felt CJ's hips quiver even more, and her hands were running through her hair more tightly as she continued to suck. To the artist, it sounded like her model was trying to stifle a scream, clenching her jaw down tight. She grunted, and then her hips spasmed into Emilee's face.

Lifting up from between her legs, Emilee pulled CJ close for a sloppy kiss right on the mouth. The women mixed spit, charcoal, sweat, and more. It felt hot, and also felt like the beginning of something.

Emilee nodded towards the door, which was now empty. "Guess we scared *him* away," she chuckled.

CJ looked over her shoulder. "Not surprising. Typical *boy*. A brief glimpse of women enjoying themselves without a cock, and they freak, run for the hills." She looked up to the ceiling, but shouted to Troy next door. *"Hope you enjoyed the show, asshole!"*

Emilee laughed. She curled up on top of CJ's damp naked chest, like a cat finding just the right spot to relax. She enjoyed listening to the pulse of her heartbeat, feeling the tide of their breathing slow down and get into sync.

"So," she said. "Uh, that was...*fun.*"

Though invisible, Emilee could feel CJ smirk. "Yeah. That was 'fun,' Em."

"Sorry." She swallowed, and then tried again. "So....what do we do *now?*"

CJ lifted up Emilee's head, so they could see each other.

"Don't you need more drawings?"

Emilee let out a dramatic sigh. "Fuck. Yeah. Yeah, you 're right. Those first sketches you let me do of you earlier were great, they really were, but you're totally right, I should start working on--".

CJ smiled, shaking her head.

"What?"

With one index finger, CJ traced a design across the surface of Emilee's skin, just below the neck. The artist's breathing got heavier, lower, and she felt her nipples getting hard again.

"Didn't you say...*everything is a drawing...?*"

Em closed her eyes, enjoying CJ's touch as her hand went beneath her shirt.

"Yeah...?" she managed to get out.

"So," CJ said, kissing her on her face to emphasize each word, "why don't we clean up, take a little study break, and then you can continue to prove this... interesting theory of yours." CJ lifted Emilee up so that they were both standing inside the studio together. "Don't you want to see how far things can go," she asked.

Emilee blinked, but her eyes were as wide open as her smile. "Yeah. Yes," she said, pulling CJ closer to her. "I do."

JUST FOR YOU

"*H*ere," Dexter said. "Take this."
He handed what looked like a hand-rolled cigarette to his boyfriend, Isaac.

"What's this?" he asked.

"Just smoke it," Jenny said. "It will make you feel that the world stopped just for you."

The three students were in the costume shop of the visual and performing arts building of their little college in Southern Vermont. Saturday night. To get here, one took a meandering trail opposite the one to the main academic buildings on campus, which connected to the residences, the Great Lawn, and the edge which everyone on campus called "the end of the world." Unless there was a play or a concert coming up, this part of the campus was generally dead. Especially on a Saturday night. And especially *this* Saturday night, as the students at Dewey House were holding their big Dress To Get Laid party.

Dexter, Jenny, and Isaac had never had any intention

in going. They had already made other plans for what they wanted to do instead.

"I can't believe we're actually *doing* this," Isaac said.

"What, you want to stop?" Jenny took the laced cigarette from his fingers, and took a giant inhale, holding it in.

"No, I didn't say that."

"Because we said, *anything* you wanted for your birthday, Isaac," Jenny replied, nodding towards Dexter. "And we meant it." Finally, her slender face let out a long plume of smoke, before passing the joint on.

"Even if it is, like, *totally fucked up*," Dexter said.

"Screw you, Dex."

"Interesting word-choice there, babe," he said on the inhale.

That notorious Dress To Get Laid party seemed to pull a good crowd each semester. Especially among freshmen, which was the first and last time Jenny (a Junior) showed up there. Dexter (sophomore) and Isaac (senior) had also gone only once, quickly deciding that the whole thing was pretty tacky, and not worth repeating. But on this small campus, students still needed to find interesting things to do during their free time. Most folks preferred to go off campus and fuck around with the locals in the bar just past the north gate and down into North B. But these three had a different kind of plan tonight, one that they had been planning for weeks.

As far as they knew, no one else was in this entire building tonight. They had the run of the place, the kind of privacy they required for their little "event". Everyone else was in Dewey.

Well, *almost* everyone. Jenny told the guys ten minutes

ago that she thought she saw a light on in one of the downstairs studios. When she pulled up in her old Toyota Celica in the back parking lot, carrying a few final costume pieces in her arms for their private party, she recognized Troy's pick-up truck. It was parked with its back facing the door, its flatbed crammed with an explosion of metal of all sizes and shapes. When she had told the boys about it, they shrugged. Even if there were other people in the building, they concluded, they were far enough away from the costume shop for it to matter.

"You still want to do this?" Jenny asked.

"Oh, fuck yeah," Isaac said. "Absolutely."

"Good," Dexter said. "Because I mean, I *love* you and all, but this....?"

"Shut up," Jenny said, elbowing him playfully in the ribs before taking the cigarette from him. "This is going to be hot."

"Hot. And fucking *wrong.*" Isaac smiled. "Just the way I like it."

Isaac sat at a make-up table, facing a mirror lined with lights. It was designed specifically for designers to work with actors and get their look just right, and Jenny had sat him down there to do the finishing touches on his costume. He wore an argyle sweater vest beneath a tweed coat, khaki pants, and brown penny loafers. In his reflection, a clarinet stood vertically on its bell. Jenny shifted her gaze back and forth, between the back of his head and looking at his reflection, combing and sculpting his naturally curly hair. Then, as a final touch, she placed a pair of glasses with thick lenses onto the bridge of his nose. She stood there, waiting for him to respond to his role.

Isaac had become early nineties Woody Allen.

"Perfect," he said. "This is *perfect*, Jen. Thank you."

"Hey. Your birthday? Your fantasy."

He gave her an air kiss, and then watched her work her magic with his boyfriend.

Dexter's costume was a bit more elaborate. A living portrait in white, he stood shrouded in folds of robes, a small cape draped over his shoulders. Jenny helped him tuck his hair under the white zucchetto crowning his skull. Like Isaac, he also wore a pair of glasses. But unlike Woody, Dexter's were thin and gold.

Dexter, dressed as Pope Pius XII, extended his arms out to the side, awaiting a reaction.

"Nice," Isaac said, applauding.

"You like?"

This year, Isaac's 21st birthday coincided with the Dress to Get Laid party, and for a present he had wanted to do something different. One night last month, after taking way too many drugs and drinking way too much vodka, he had confessed a fantasy to his two closest friends that was as outrageous as it was specific. The next morning, even after the hangover and the detox had passed, though, Isaac couldn't stop thinking of it. So he told Dex and Jen that he was serious: that what he really wanted this year for his twenty-first was some filthy cosplay. I mean, if not *here*, where else was Isaac going to be able to live out this sexual role-play?

His roommate Jenny was the costume shop manager, so she knew how to collect whatever costumes and props they'd need. She took to planning for it like any show she had worked on, not seeming to blink at how nasty and intimate this one was. Isaac learned that she had been secretly accumulating costume pieces from the College's recent production of *Marat/Sade,* as some of those were going to be perfect for their little party. She was in from word go. Jenny adored her roommate, and thought Isaac's fantasy would be fun. When asked if she had ever done anything like this before, she shrugged and showed her big toothy smile. "Isn't that what college was for," she said. "Experimenting?"

When Isaac told his boyfriend Dexter, he didn't seem that fazed by the fantasy, either. Rather than disgust or horror, he just responded with a laugh. It was one of the things he loved most about Dex: give him enough pot, suck his dick often enough, and basically he was game for just about anything.

Dexter/Pope Pius XII came forward, standing behind Isaac/Woody. He lifted his arms in a snarky imitation of the crucifixion.

"Well," he asked, "what do you think, babe?"

"Mmmmm," Isaac crooned, smiling at his boyfriend's reflection. "Love it! Is yours comfortable?"

"Oh yeah, totally," he said, grinning like a cat. "Jen did a great job, making sure it all fit just right. In all the right places." He gave her a wink and pointed his index finger towards her.

"Unsolicited praise will get you far in this world, Dexter," she said, taking off her sweater. She was now wearing only a black lace bra. "Thank you, just the same."

Dexter made the sign of the cross in the air before her. His profane benediction elicited a laugh from his boyfriend, who almost spat out the glass of red wine he had just poured. "May God bless you, my child," he said solemnly.

Jenny kicked off her pants. Standing nearly naked

wearing only her underwear, she gave the Pope the finger. "That's *Goddess* to you, faggot."

Dexter laughed. "Of course, right. *Mea culpa,* you fuckin' breeder!"

She stood on the balls of her feet to kiss him on the cheek, then turned to Isaac. "Now. What do you think of our birthday boy, here?"

"I love it!" he exclaimed. "Like, full-on *Annie Hall.*"

"Oh," Jenny pouted. "I was going more for *Crimes and Misdemeanors.*"

"I love it," Isaac said, turning to her. It looked like he was going to cry. "Really. I can't thank you enough."

Jenny bent forward and kissed him playfully on the mouth. She gave his bottom lip a little nibble before standing back up.

"Are you kidding? You don't have to thank me. I can't wait!" She turned to Dexter. "*We* can't wait. Your present is one all of us can enjoy!"

"That's right, babe," Dexter said. "It's all for you. But, y 'know, like Jenny said, all for *us* too. Heh heh."

Dexter lifted Isaac's head, and then began sharing a deep kiss.

"Hey, hey, HEY, boys," Jenny said, pushing past them. "Wait for me! I have to get *my* costume on!" She ran deeper into the costume shop, her bare feet slapping against the linoleum floor.

"Then *hustle*, Jen," Dexter said, putting his thumb into Isaac's mouth to suck. "I'm gonna make him regret marrying Soon-Yi! Ha ha! We're gonna, like, speak in tongues, and whatever!"

Jenny squealed with delight from the bowels of the costume shop. In the half shadow, Dexter saw her hurriedly putting her legs into some baggy black pants with suspenders.

"Hey," Isaac said, turning around in the chair to look up at the Pope. "Forgive me, Father, for I have sinned. It's been....well, actually, this is my *first* confession."

"I thought Jews didn't believe in sin," he replied "Especially neurotic New Yorkers like you, Woody."

"I guess--I guess it's all that Dostoevski I read during my formative years," he replied, doing a pretty good Woody Allen impersonation. "Raskolnikov. Morality. Crime and punishment, y'know? And--."

Jenny let out a big groan. She was pulling black gloves up her slender pale arms, all the way up to her biceps."Yo, Pope! Put something into the pie-hole of that nebbish. He's talking *way* too much."

Dexter's stiff cock was already tenting beneath his papal cassock. He first put his index finger into Woody's mouth, who began sucking with fervor. The Pope rolled his eyes into the back of his head, tilting his head up and back to the silent heavens. Isaac really tugged on him with strong motions back and forth, rhythmically, like a bird pecking with its beak. The Pope then took his supplicant's hand and placed it over his straining cock beneath the fabric.

"Your own....personal...*Jesus...*," he sang quietly. "Heh. Now rub it, baby. Suck it."

While continuing to steadily swallow the finger of Hitler's Pope, Woody began to rub his stiff erection at the same time. Dexter's hips began pulsing forward and back, coaxing his boyfriend to follow his lead and get into the rhythm. It was growing hot in the costume shop; there were few windows here. The signature thick glasses completing the costume of the infamous filmmaker were starting to slip down his nose. Isaac reached to take them off.

"Ah ah ah!" the Pope scolded, wagging his free hand. "Keep those on. Did I say you could take those off, Woody? Ha! Didn't think so!"

"I think he needs a little punishment, don´t you, Your Holiness?" Jenny said. When she returned to the room with the two guys, she had completely transformed, too. She strode elegantly, like a dancer. Her baggy pants hung from suspenders over her bare shoulders, her torso completely naked except for her long black gloves. She covered her breasts with the palms of her hands, and atop her head tilted a black SS officer captain´s hat.

Jenny was dressed as Lucia, Charlotte Rampling´s character from *Night Porter*.

Pushing Woody away, the Pope freed his finger from Woody's wet mouth, quickly unfastening the rope which kept his pants up. After they fell to the floor, he stepped his bare legs out of them, then pointed to the floor in front of his toes.

"Kneel before God, Sodomite," he commanded. Rising from his chair, Woody crossed to sit on his knees before the Pope. The bottom of Dexter´s cassock still covered his waist, so the Pope guided Isaac's head underneath his robe, giving plenty of room for his boyfriend to swallow his St. Peter. Woody began sucking on his wood.

"Eets unt uhn-fair," Lucia whined in a ridiculous parody of a German accent. "I vant to zee."

The Pope lifted the hem of his garment and clutched it between the fangs of his teeth. Lucia played with her own nipples while leaning up against the wall, enjoying seeing

Woody suck. She found it hot, watching a man suck another man's dick, and had always got off to gay porn way more than straight porn. Jenny didn't know why this was, and didn't really care if she never knew the answer. Right now, she was focused on teasing the tips of her nipples with her gloved fingers, enjoying the feel of the silk on bare flesh. From her vantage point, here up against the wall, she was getting off watching her two friends get off. Everyone was happy.

Now, Pope Pius looked down at the top of Woody's head, bobbing forward and back. He liked the feeling of how his cock was sliding super slow into his mouth, how his boyfriend was really using his tongue, being in control of every single sensation. Maybe it was his role as pontiff, but Dexter became impatient after a while, and began pumping his hips faster towards the back of Woody's throat. He always got turned on hearing his boyfriend gag, whenever Isaac went down on him. He'd asked him about this before, if it was okay or if it hurt, when they had first started hooking up freshman year. Isaac said he didn't mind it when his boyfriend got a little more aggressive during sex. And secretly, though he would never admit it to anyone, Dexter always felt somewhat ashamed for getting hard during the times his lover choked on his cock. What did that say about him, and his fucked up sexuality?

"Oh yeah," the Pope exclaimed, tilting his head back with pleasure. "That's so fucking good, babe!"

"Is he better than Soon-Yi, Woody?" Lucia asked, twisting her own nipples until she winced. Isaac responded with some sort of affirmative sound, but it was hard to tell for sure. His mouth was currently cock-stuffed.

Jenny slinked her way forward, desiring to be closer to the two boys. Sliding one hand down between her legs, she gripped Dexter's cheeks with one of her gloved hands.

"So exciting, seeing you two get it on," she said, locking his eyes with hers. "I don't know why all of this turns me on so much. And you know what? I don't really give a fuck."

Behind her, Jenny heard a voice, shouting. It sounded like it came from the other side of the building, where all the visual art studios were. It sound like someone had said, *"Hope you enjoyed the show, asshole!"*

What the fuck? Did someone just yell that? In front of her, the Pope was continuing to face-fuck the pedo, so maybe she had just made that up. Weird.

Lucia looked down at Woody, her eyes gliding down his back. Taking the clarinet off of the table, she silently arranged his body so that his hands were behind his back and near his waist.

"Hold this," she commanded, putting the instrument into his upturned palms. "And then get up. On your feet."

His head continued to work Dexter's penis beneath the holy cassock, but it was awkward standing up. Issac stumbled along the way to verticality, before he bent forward from the waist. His hands remained clutching Woody's trademark woodwind behind him, while Dexter guided his head up and down with strong hands. The Pope began bouncing his head up and down, creating a pleasure so keen through his rod that Dexter feared that his teeth might tear through the fabric.

Jenny, meanwhile, pulled down Isaac's pants and

underwear, letting them bunch over his ankles. His bare bottom, so white and round, appeared almost feminine. She took off one of her long black gloves, twisted it, then folded it in half. Wielding it like a riding crop, she struck his ass, smiling as his hips and flesh quivered at the impact. A tiny red welt bloomed from the surface of the skin on his right cheek.

"C'mon," Lucia grunted, striking his ass again. "Fuckin ´ pervert. Suck that dick."

Dexter pulled his robe up and over his head. He wasn't really into girls, not since his first and only girlfriend in high school, but he had always liked Jenny since coming to college. And right now, with her whole Charlotte Rampling meets dominatrix thing going on, he found her power and confidence really hot. Without thinking about it, he reached over Woody's sweaty back and extended his hand towards Lucia´s mouth. Her mouth pulsed and sucked over three of his fingers, and her eyes blazed with dark desire beneath the brim of that Nazi cap of hers. Dexter felt his cock grow even harder inside his boyfriend's mouth. *Damn,* he thought. *I'm a sick mother-fucker, aren't I?*

Lucia struck their little birthday fuck toy again, rhyth-mically.

"Oh shit," the Pope gasped. "Jesus fucking *Christ.*"

"What do you think?" she asked, pulling Dexter´s finger out of her mouth. "You think our birthday boy is ready for the rest of his present?"

Isaac moaned something, and Dexter slowed his sucking mouth over his stiff cock to just the way he wanted it. Giving Woody´s bare butt one last thwack of her glove, Jenny smiled when she saw the thin red lines run diagonally across his ass. A little barcode of pain and pleasure. From the nearby makeup table she pulled open a drawer, revealing a bottle of lubricant and a strapon dildo that Isaac had given her in preparation for his birthday. The two of them had gone together to purchase it earlier that month during a weekend trip to New York; it was some place down in the Village, off of Christopher Street. When they entered, they went to the counter to ask for help, and found a store clerk that looked like a librarian with a filthy mind. After listening to what they were looking for, she directed them to the top shelf. She recommended one just thick enough to not hurt Isaac *too* much, while at the same time make sure Jenny got off. Holding the strapon in her hands just in front of her own pelvis, she showed Jenny how it all worked with a smile. Behind the silicone shaft, right at the base, lay a small triangle.

"Every time you bang your boyfriend, or whatever," the dirty librarian explained, winking towards Isaac, "you 'll get a little bang too. Right there on your clit."

In the college costume shop, attaching the strapon felt to Jenny like putting on a tool belt; Lucia didn't need to take off her fascist costume, thankfully. She adjusted the phallus until it stood at attention just over the top of her vulva, then squirted some goop from the bottle into the palm of her gloved hand. She immediately began rubbing it all around Woody´s puckered little asshole. Pulling up from sucking Dexter´s cock, Isaac let out a howl.

"Oh *yes*," he screamed. "Fuck me. *Fuck me*, you fuckin´ Nazi!"

"Oh don´t worry, piggy," Lucia said, lathering her

phallus with some lube now. "I'm gonna fuck you harder than the Holocaust."

The Pope laughed. "Get back to work, Woody. Ha! Suck my woody... *Woody.*" Holding the back of his boyfriend's head, he put his mouth over his rod and his staff, to comfort him, just as Lucia thrust her shaft deep inside his ass.

Jenny wasn't gentle or namby-pamby with her role. Holding onto Woody's hips firmly, she immediately began pumping. No marathon for Lucia, but a sprint--just as Isaac had instructed her as part of his fantasy. Dexter got even more turned on, watching her ride his boyfriend: how the muscles in her arms and shoulders remained taught, while her small breasts shook; how her hips furiously drove the phallus deeper inside Isaac's ass. Beneath the brim of her evil officer's cap, she looked into the eyes of the Pope with malevolent glee, and her teeth bit into her bottom lip like a wolf.

Isaac was making more choking sounds than usual tonight, so Dexter lifted up his lover's face until his back was arched and the two could look into each other's eyes. Woody kept grasping the clarinet behind his back, and Lucia held the center of the horn one-handed like some crazy cowgirl riding a bull. Dexter kissed his lover's forehead, and then slapped him hard across the face.

"Are you sorry, Woody?" the Pope asked gently. Isaac's ass strained to keep up with the intensity of Jenny's thrusting dildo, which worked him harder and faster. Dexter spat into his lover's mouth, and then slapped his face a second time. "I said, *are you sorry?* Huh? I need to hear you confess, you piece of shit."

"Yes," Isaac whimpered. "Yes, OW! Ohhhh fuck, OH FUCK. It's so deep….".

"Yes, indeed," he agreed. "She's a *good* fucking fascist, isn't she?"

Lucia slapped Woody's ass, hard, and Dexter could practically see a red handprint glow over his lover's buttocks. She slapped him again without breaking her speed at all. *What a sexy bitch,* he thought.

"Hey! Your Holiness?" she panted, getting a good work out from her furious fucking. "Shut that motherfucker up. I don't want this creep to talk. I want him to *come.*"

"Fuckin'-a-right."

The Pope plunged his cock back into Woody's mouth, and Lucia stormed her phony dick even further. She arched her chest forward, exposing her naked tits even more under Dexter's gaze, and Isaac whimpered from being double-fucked from both ends. He tried his best to hold onto the clarinet, but he felt like he was going to fall, so he grabbed onto his boyfriend's hips, which continued pumping into his mouth. The musical instrument exploded into three parts on the floor, the clatter overcome by the howling laughter.

"Come on, *come* on," Jenny coached her roommate, whose butt cheeks spread open before the strap-on's hilt. "It's what you wanted, right? *Right?*"

Reaching down and under Woody's waist, Jenny grabbed Isaac's erect cock with the kind of detached precision of someone milking a cow. Almost instantaneously, she felt him spurt his hot spunk onto her fingers. His scream of pleasure was muffled by Dexter's grunts, as the Pope's hips strained into a spasm which unleashed into his boyfriend's mouth. Isaac did his best to swallow every drop of it for his birthday, as he had been fantasizing about this for weeks, but he had to pull off. Atop trembling legs, he hacked some of Dexter's cum onto the floor of the costume shop, his mouth only able to take maybe at least half of it. While he remained hunched over, hands on knees, panting and groaning, Jenny slowly withdrew her phallus, causing him to hiss with sweet agony. Unfastening the belt before letting it fall to the floor, she stroked his lower back tenderly in tiny little circles.

"Whew," he said, standing up, his legs continuing to quiver. "God *damn!*"

"Happy birthday," Jenny said.

Dexter laughed first, and then the three of them went into a jag of giggles. The intensity of the scene, the giddiness of a private fantasy being realized, created a sweet lightness within the dark rows of theatrical clothing. After placing his fake crucifix over his boyfriend's neck, Dexter kissed him sweetly. "How was it, babe? Did we do okay? Was it everything you fantasized about?"

"Oh, fuck yeah," Isaac said, hugging him and crying with tears of gratitude. "Better!"

"I was afraid that we were pounding you too hard, there--"

"No no no," Isaac said. He turned to Jenny—his roommate, his best friend, and now...his lover, too? He gave her a giant hug, and said into her shoulder. "I told you: I wanted it rough, *fraulein.*"

She smiled, then placed the SS cap on Isaac's head. "That's Führer to you, babycakes!"

"Oh man," Isaac laughed. "I'm *never* gonna forget this

night. Ever. This is, like...the best birthday of my entire life."

"So far," Dexter said, pulling him close.

"Oh shit! Wait!" Jenny said. "I almost forgot."

Dexter and Isaac were still kissing lovingly in the middle of the costume shop when Jenny returned with her Nikon, already assembled on top of her tripod. Placing it about 10 feet away from them, she set up the timer.

"It's going to be a little dark in here, but--".

"Don't worry about it," Isaac said. "It's going to be *just right*."

"Say cheese!" Dexter added.

Jenny stepped back to join her friends, the three standing in all of their sweat and beauty, the debris of the silent clarinet around their feet:

Woody stood in the middle, of course, his pants still tangled around his ankles, his glasses miraculously still atop the bridge of his nose. Around his neck, a gold cross; and crowning his head, a Nazi hat.

To his left, the Pope stood naked and smiling, his arm squeezing his boyfriend's shoulder.

And to his right, Lucia, covering her bare breasts with her fingertips, her lips puckered into an air kiss towards the camera.

WHITE

*B*ret should have brought a warmer coat. In
fact, *any coat at all* would have been a good
fucking idea.

Technically, tonight was the beginning of spring. But
apparently that little memo yet to reach Southern
Vermont, as snow and ice continued to linger and over-
stay their welcome here. He wondered how he could have
forgotten the long winters here, as he blew into his
cupped hands, hoping his breath would warm them up.

Despite numerous invitations to do so, it had been
years since Bret had set foot on the grounds of his alma
mater. Was it this cold when he was a student her? Maybe
this just was another sign of climate change. Or maybe,
and probably the most likely explanation, he couldn't
remember huge swaths of his college experience because
he was so cranked up on coke and vodka back then.

Back then, he smirked. *As if the place has changed.*

Closing the top button of his black long-sleeved shirt,
Bret zipped up the front of his hoodie (also black) as high

as it would go. Though cold, he kept the hood itself down, not wanting to mess up his haircut. He embraced the wind's subtle punishment against the top of his ears, which felt covered in frost. Pressing his Ray-Bans higher up the bridge of his nose, he looked back over his shoulder at his rental car parked by the side of the curving country road, its hazard lights flashing like a tiny space-ship. He checked his phone again, seeing if it would turn on, but the screen was still cracked. He had dropped it by accident when he got out of the car to check out the flat tire twenty minutes ago. Tucking the phone into his front pockets on his pants (yep, you guessed it—also black), he began marching up the hill and through the darkness. His quest for a telephone was now afoot.

Bret stepped off the shoulder alongside the road and onto the path leading to the North Gate. Once on the path of dried mud, Bret veered right. There was a small on-campus bar just up the way, serving only beer and wine, but he thought he remembered from his college days that they had a pay phone. He'd make his call, grab a quick drink, and then meet Triple-A down by his car. And if not...well, one thing at a time.

Early on in the college's history, the North Gate led to a train stop that would shuttle students, faculty, and locals between Vermont and New York. These days however, that was but a ghostly memory, and the nearest Amtrak stop was all the way over in Albany. These days, this path leading away from the campus was used for folks who didn't want to drive down to North B, who didn't mind a half mile walk down the hill to grab beer and burger at Kevin's. Before his tire blew out, Bret had debated going back there, to see if he could woo the bartender with his words and score one more drink before driving back down to New York. But the owner of Kevin´s had made it abundantly clear before they pointed him towards the door: he was not welcome there. *Never been eighty-sixed from a New England bar,* he thought, shrugging his shoulders. He had been through far worse in his life. Initially, the flat tire had pissed him off, but when he realized how close he was to the college, he adapted, got over it. Surely he´d find a phone somewhere on the campus, right? Even if it was after midnight? College campuses don't usually fall asleep this early. Especially not this one.

Walking along the desolate foot path, Bret didn't see any living creatures around him, human or animal. If there were any there, they remained hidden in the darkness and below the dome of the cicadas´ eerie music. *Perfect place for a murder,* he smiled to himself, *or at least an early eighties version of one.* "Friday the 13th: Part Whatever" would be perfect here, he thought, with its forests of deep green. The remote location of the college reminded Bret of how cut off he and everyone else on the campus was from the rest of civilization here, how far from safety and any contact with the outside world. *It really is at the end of the world,* the mused, watching his breath cloud in front of his face. Even when he was a student here, Bret sensed a palpable spookiness about the place, a kind of atmosphere of black magic which made him and his friends feel like anything could happen, that everything was permissable. Some of his classmates attributed this vibe to the College being on indigenous land, an unusual spot where the "four winds meet," according to the Mohicans. Being from Brentwood and having lived most of his life in L.A. and New York, Bret never held too much stock in those kinds of things. In his opinion, the reason why the college was fucked up was due to all of the available drugs, combined with the constant hunger for sex and the removal of any boundaires.

He hoped, with the change into a new millennium, that those precious qualities of the college hadn't changed.

Bret heard the bar before he could actually see the dark brown wood of its barn-like shape. Some track by Eminem, from his newest album, blasted from inside. He respected Mathers´ in-your-face, I-don´t-give-a-shit atti-tude; he felt like the two of them were kindred spirits, in a way. As he got closer to the entrance, a pair of what looked to be college kids spilled out of the bar´s front door. And while they were not Jason Voorhees or Michael Meyers, what they were wearing costumes would defi-nitely qualify to some as horrific.

The young woman wore a nurse's uniform, Bret supposed, but only the kind required if she worked the night shift at the Playboy Mansion. Her flared white skirt barely covered the globes of her firm round ass, and her bare legs had the slender strength of a dancer´s. Her blonde hair was tucked back into a white cap emblazoned with a cross matching her fire-engine red lipstick, and the front of her white blouse was unzipped down to the navel, exposing a silver bellybutton ring on otherwise smooth bare skin. When she moved, Bret glimpsed black X´s of duct tape covering her nipples, a punk rock slut´s idea of underwear. Bret immediately thought she was cool.

Her companion was a young guy wearing what Bret guessed were faux leather pants. His hairless torso was completely bare except for a dog collar around his neck studded with metal. A carrot top, the guy´s hair was cropped short, like some sort of military crew-cut. Bret licked his lips, looking at the cinnamon- freckles peppering the boy´s muscular back, and concluded that this kid spent most of his time lifting weights and not reading books. A long metal leash connected Leather Boy ´s collar, on one end, to a tangle of silver held in the hand of the Slut Nurse, on the other. The overhead lamp perched over the bar´s entrance made the chain connecting the two of them glint like some long line of spit. Bret privately confirmed to himself that yes, the hand of Slut Nurse did indeed have red fingernails, matching her lipstick. In her other hand was a flip phone, which she pressed close to the side of her face. Her eyes widened in horror, and then she began shouting.

"Well where the fuck did they *go?*"

Her voice was unmistakably West Coast, definitely Southern California. If Bret had to guess, he'd say she had grown up somewhere in Sherman Oaks before coming to college here. Though a generation apart, he felt like he knew her, just from her brief bark into the phone. Seeing her was like seeing himself, though maybe through the glass of a funhouse mirror. Her pose was his, and onto her Bret projected his own qualities, then and now: the detached affect, the unpredictable behavior, the aura of sexual indulgence yet to come. This slutty nurse girl probably practiced being a total ice queen in front of the mirror in her dorm room; she might even practice more when she went to eat in the dining hall, or when walking across the Great Lawn between classes. Just like Bret did, when he was a student here. It was important to rehearse, for when you had to chew other assholes out, like this fucker on the other end of her phone. Based on the one side Bret could hear, the Nurse was angry because her re-up–or her boyfriend (he wasn't sure if they were not one and the same)--had bailed on meeting up tonight. Instead of staying on campus to party with her and her pet, the man on the other end of the line went AWOL. Most likely with someone else, Bret figured. And now she was here, stranded on campus on Saturday night, alone with the Leather Boy–less than a man and more like a living toy.

Clicking her phone shut, the Nurse inhaled, and then yelled uselessly to the full moon, which had decided just at that moment to reveal its indifferent face from behind the bruised-dark clouds.

"FUUUUUUCK!"

Suddenly, like a magician, she produced a cigarette. Leather Boy immediately pulled a book of matches from an unseen pocket near his crotch, and frantically attempted to strike a flame for her. Bret frowned at this bizarre theater: this near-impossible task was made even more difficult with the gusts of the four winds meeting. *Wonder if that matchbook was damp*, he wondered. *Was there any sweat there, in between his legs?* Wetting his lips with his tongue, he began to smile at the image, like a shark suddenly smelling blood in the water.

And then, miraculously, a feeble flame. Leather Boy´s hands protected it with his cup-shaped hands, offering it reverently to the Nurse. She bent forward slightly, revealing her full and nearly-bare-breasts, her full lips surrounding the filter of the white cigarette like the stem of a lollipop. She sucked. When she raised her head, a long plume of smoke rose into the cold night. Bret surmised that the Nurse enjoyed watching Leather Boy struggle with these idiotic tasks, such as lighting a match for her outside on this windy night. In fact, based on how her hard nipples strained against the duct tape, Bret guessed that failure and humiliation gave her a rush.

Hand on her hip, head cocked, the Nurse now shifted her attention formally towards Bret.

"What the fuck are you supposed to be," she smirked.

"What do you mean?"

"Your clothes," the Nurse said, raising her eyebrows. "You look....well, pretty fucking *ordinary,* if you ask me. Don't you know what tonight is?"

Bret looked down at his clothes. Below a black hoodie, he wore the same pair of pants he purchased two (maybe three) years ago. Thin argyle socks and a pair of black Vans did their best to keep his feet warm against the cold. Along with his gaze, he lifted his palms back up to the Nurse and Leather Boy. Bret was about to reply with a snarky-casual remark when three people burst out from the bar. A young woman led two men, one in each hand, towards the houses and the Great Lawn. All were in a hurry, the two guys like little puppies in her wake. She was around the same age as the Nurse, but her hair was long and dark, and her skin was practically porcelain. Instead of a slutty nurse's uniform, this woman wore a black leather corset, emphasizing her giant tits and the roundness of her ass. One of the two boys looked a bit older, but both wore clothes that were pretty ordinary and bland: worn blue jeans, jackets. The two eagerly followed her lead, and the three disappeared into the night. The Nurse enjoyed another drag from her cigarette before Bret put two and two together.

"Oh," Bret said, putting his hand to his forehead. "Let me guess: tonight is Dress to Get Laid?"

"Finally," she sighed, blowing smoke towards him. Leather Boy began to laugh derisively, but his voice was suddenly truncated, making his giggle sound more like the yelp of a dog. The Nurse had stabbed the heel of her white leather boot into the top of his toes.

"Hey, sorry," Bret said, "I didn't realize. I was just....".

"What?"

"Looking for a phone, actually. My car," he gestured vaguely behind him. "Flat."

She tapped the ash off the end of her cigarette, and Leather Boy immediately knelt before her. Cupping his hands over his head, he now contorted himself into a human ashtray.

"You go here?"

Bret's smile widened like that of a Great White, and shook his head. "Used to,"

"Figured," she said with a wink. "Thought you looked kinda old."

Leather Boy tried to laugh again, but the Nurse jabbed her heel into his thigh this time. Another yelp from him. Another smile from me.

"So? What's *your* story?"

"What do you mean?"

"Well," Bret said, shrugging his shoulders, "based on what I overheard from your earlier phone call, sounds like...you got screwed."

"I wish," she said. "I mean, you're *right*. I *did* get screwed. Out of *getting* screwed. If you know what I mean."

Bret smiled, amused by her attempt at cleverness, her

undergraduate humor. So desperate to sound adult, even though she was probably living at home with her parents less than five years ago. Was *he* like that, he wondered, when *he* was her age and going to school here? Working that hard to sound and appear jaded and cynical about everything? Yeah, probably.

"Yeah," Bret said. "I know what you mean."

He took a step closer, joining them in the pool of pale yellow light falling from the lamp above the bar entrance. He pulled out a pack of cigarettes from the pocket of his hoodie. Before he could get his Zippo out to light it, though,, Leather Boy scooted his knees along the pavement, trying to get closer to him. He reprised his earlier performance of desperately trying to light a match, before the next gust of wind went through. Bret paused, his thumb on his lighter's metallic wheel, and looked to the Nurse.

"What happens if I just...light my own cigarette?"

She shrugged. "He'll be disappointed," she replied with a smile. "Or I'll

punish him. Either way, he'll enjoy it. It's his thing. Being submissive turns him on."

"And being on top is your jam," he replied. It wasn't a question.

Bret turned to look at Leather Boy, who had gotten another match lit. Kid was good at this. As before, he swiftly cupped his hands to protect it from the Four Winds. When it got close to his mouth, Bret leaned forward and blew it out. Leather Boy dropped his hands with defeat.

"Ooops," Bret said sarcastically. He then lit his own cigarette with a flick from his Zippo.

"Oooh, you are *bad,*" the Nurse said with a husky laugh.

"You don't even know the half of it," he said, trying to blow the smoke towards the Boy without being too obvious about it. "So what's this ´punishment´? Can I watch?"

"Maybe," she replied. "Or maybe you could...do more."

"Well, I want to do *something.* ´Cuz right now, I´m just freezing my ass off."

The Nurse nodded her head. "Follow me. I know a place not far."

"Cool. Let's go. This place is dead."

The Nurse stubbed out the end of her cigarette into one of the Leather Boy´s open palms. He winced and gritted his teeth, but held his hand in place until it was out. *Impressive,* Bret thought. Before turning to lead them away, she tugged his leash, yanking him forward by the collar around his neck.

"Where are we going?," Bret asked.

"Near the End of the World," she said, without looking back.

———

THE LONG STRETCH of grass that formed the Great Lawn of the college was surrounded by buildings, forming a kind of horseshoe. Old New England houses for students and even a few faculty ran along either side. The main building, which held classes, administrative offices, and the dining hall, sat at the top of the horseshoe; while opposite, all the way down at the lawn´s bottom-most edge, was what everyone called the End of the World.

The center of the college's campus, on a clear day one could see a beautiful stretch of rolling mountains from this point, with maybe a farmhouse or a grain silo dotting the slopes of green. At night, of course, one could see much much less. There was no light pollution here in the southern tip of the Green Mountain State; this was not like New York or Los Angeles. Here, Bret thought, you could actually still see the stars.

As well as a few ghosts. As Bret followed the Nurse and Leather Boy on their forward trajectory, walking deeper into whatever mystery lay ahead, he occasionally saw other students stumbling across their path in the lunar dark. Their bodies criss-crossed the lawn, moving from one house to the other like harmless specters, their feet crunching the cold grass with an audible crunch. He probably could have seen more of their faces if he took off his Ray Bans, but Bret liked this little trip of his. It was like giving himself a private little challenge: how far could he walk through this night, without taking them off? Besides, his sunglasses felt like a key to some part of his identity. Maybe *this* was his costume for tonight, for the college party celebrating the lonely and the horny. If she was the Nurse and he was Leather Boy, what was he?

"Hey," he said. "I forgot to ask. What's your name?"

"I'm Donna," the Nurse said.

"Are you serious?"

She looked over at him, confused. "Yeah. Why?"

"Let me guess. Leather Boy here is named Jonathan?"

She stopped, and turned towards him. "How did you know?"

Bret shook his head and smiled. "Nevermind. We almost there?"

"Yeah, just through here."

She began to veer right, heading towards Welling House. Or maybe it was Bingham? Bret always got them confused, even when he was a student here. He began to veer towards the main entrance, opposite the End of the World, but Donna instead pulled Leather Boy towards a window on the ground floor. She leaned her ear towards the glass, listening to the dark. Bret stubbed out his cigarette onto the grass.

"What the fuck are we doing?"

"Shhh," she commanded. Donna snapped her fingers, and Jonathan shape-shifted again. This time, instead of a human ashtray, his posture resembled a guard dog, his bare back to the building, his eyes looking out. Crouching down, the top of Leather Boy's head remained below the edge of the windowsill. He began slowly swiveling his eyes back and forth from the direction they had just come, his body motionless. Despite his lack of clothing, he calmly and intently looked for movement, seeing if anyone was approaching their small group. *Scanning,* Bret thought, and remembered how much he enjoyed that Cronenberg movie with Michael Ironside.

"Give me a boost," Donna said.

Bending his knees, Bret interlaced his hands, creating a place for her to take a step. When she lifted up and off of the ground, his face met her crotch. Donna was naked from the waist down, her tiny white mini-skirt the only thing separating his nose from her pussy. She smelled like a new flower, some kind of fresh fruit. Her second step, which she placed on top of Bret's shoulder, was a little more intense. Her boot's heel dug into his shoulder, causing Bret to bite down on his bottom lip silently. Then, softly, Donna's weight left him, and he looked up, getting a perfect view of her bare legs and ass. For the first time this night, Bret slid his sunglasses up his forehead, double-checking to make sure. *Yep,* he thought, *that girl is indeed naked.* He let out a whistle, and made a loud kissing sound.

"Creep," she said, without looking down.

Scaling the side of the house, Donna made her way to the second floor, where a window was open. With a soft grunt, she pushed the sill up more, then slid her body headfirst into the darkened room. Before she disappeared, Bret saw her bare butt cheeks catch the moonlight for a second, like an inverted valentine.

He looked down at Leather Boy, whose head continued to be on guard duty, slowly rotating his head left and right.

"What the fuck is she doing?"

His canine-like companion didn't even bark a reply. Bret was about to light another cigarette, when something hard landed on the top of his head.

A knotted piece of fabric. Looking up, he saw a rope made out of mismatched bed sheets descending from the second-story window. Donna poked her mischievous head out of the window.

"Come on, hurry," she whispered, before disappearing inside.

Shifting his stance again, Jonathan now formed a kind of step-ladder out of his body. Bret walked up one of his thighs to get up to one of his bare shoulders, feeling his muscles strain beneath his feet as he climbed up the side of the house. Reaching the window, he stepped one foot in before quickly ducking his head under the window sill.

Inside, the Nurse was just lighting a fat candle. Tugging on the rope's top end wrapped around the metal bedpost, he tossed the slack end back down to Leather Boy, then looked around.

The door room had Heterosexual Male written all over it: there were posters of De Palma's *Scarface* and the Notorious B.I.G., as well as an overflowing pile of dirty laundry in one corner. Bret hoped he wouldn't have to go to the bathroom any time soon, as he was afraid of what he might find in there. The odor in the air was a funky mix of used gym socks and old incense. In front of a wooden drawer, Donna was rummaging through drawers, opening and closing them rapidly.

"Looking for something?"

Ignoring him, she continued her search, tossing t-shirts and jeans to the floor like a seasoned DEA agent. "Percy's gone for the night. Probably getting high with that bitch, Nicole," she said bitterly. "But he's got to have some here, somewhere. He always has some."

"What?"

"Drugs," Leather Boy said behind him. Bret hadn't even heard him climbing up. The kid had the stealthy grace of an animal. Turning back to the Slut Nurse, she stood tall with a smile. In front of Bret's face she presented a plastic sandwich bag, its bottom heavy with something that looked like oregano. But of course, it wasn't.

"Ta dah," she said. "Now, let's…have some fun."

Leather Boy immediately went over to her and produced some rolling paper from somewhere. *His crotch? Again,* Bret wondered. *Did he have pockets down there, or what?* Bret watched Donna carefully pour a line of pot onto the white paper, then lick its edge with her pink tongue before twirling it all together nice and tight. Sticking one end of it into her mouth, she leaned forward towards the candle's flame, and sucked. There was a faint crackling sound as the paper burned.

"Killing a sailor," Bret said.

Looking at him, she spoke on the inhale, "Some sailors deserve to die." She then let out a huge plume of smoke, and passed him the joint.

He took a hit, and his head immediately felt emptier, more spacious. If nothing else, Donna knew how to roll a pretty sweet joint, and this weed was seriously choice. After taking another hit, Donna made the sound system light up and start pulsing something–something low with bass and beats. The groove reminded Bret of a nightclub he used to go to, down over in West Hollywood, before it got shut down over a drug bust. He offered the joint to Leather Boy, but Jonathan was already kneeling in front of Bret's crotch, his hands frantically unzipping his khakis.

Guess I'll look for a phone....after.

Taking a final toke, Bret offered the joint to Donna, who put it inside her mouth while peeling off her tiny nurse's jacket. She hung it up on a doorknob, and showed Bret her bare back while moving her tiny hips in little figure-eights. When she turned around, she wore nothing but the nurse's hat, the white boots, and the black Xs covering her nipples. She had shaved her pubic hair, and Donna's belly button ring was catching some of the candlelight. She offered him the joint again, but then pulled it back when Bret reached for it.

"Hey," he said, "what the fuck...?"

81

"Oh come on," she said, "I know you´re at least *bi-curious*. Besides, I like watching guys fuck. It turns me on."

"What about him," Bret said, looking down. Donna shrugged.

"Do whatever you want with him. He likes whatever I want him to do."

In one firm tug, Leather Boy yanked Bret´s pants and underwear firmly downward, which freed his cock. He was already erect, and his dick sprung right up to tap the lips on the boy's face. Hesitating for a second, Jonathan´s eyes bulged. He opened his jaw as wide as he could, trying to swallow Bret, but he couldn´t go further than maybe half way down.

"Jesus fucking *Christ*," Donna said, her eyes widening. "You´re fucking hung like a *horse*."

Bret chuckled, then fondled the red hair behind the kid's head. He gasped, trying to force Jonathan down more. It was hard, but felt good. "And I only wear size ten," he said.

Leather Boy began moaning and gagging, and his hands clutched Bret´s hips and ass to stay in a position best for giving head. Bret looked down at this submissive kid, this spontaneous sex slave, and decided that he was very glad that his car had gotten a flat tire tonight. Jonathan seemed to enjoy it the rougher Bret fucked his face, and so he decided to test out his little theory. Holding the back of his head with both hands now, Bret began bucking his hips forward into Leather Boy´s mouth. He found a steady rhythm, and enjoyed the feeble resistance Jonathan gave to each one of his thrusts. Leather Boy began to slap his ass cheeks, trying to tell Breet to stop; but these slaps had the opposite effect. They only turned Bret on more, inspiring him to pump his cock into his sore mouth and open throat even deeper. After the eighth or ninth time, though, Bret decided to give this punk a little break.

"Mmmmm," Donna said approvingly, "my turn."

Moving herself to him in time with the music, the Nurse lifted the edge of her tiny white skirt and opened her legs wide, before hinging forward at the waist into a deep forward bend. *Definitely a dancer,* Bret though. He kicked his khakis off his ankles, while Leather Boy crawled over to her. He pressed his nose and mouth into her crotch, lapping at her pussy like a dog drinking from his bowl of water. Donna held onto her ankles, and began writhing her hips against Jonathan's face as she rolled back up to standing. Her hands moved over herself, playing with herself, each gesture depicting an imaginary lover: she ran her fingers through her thick hair, she let a hand trail down between her breasts, she squeezed and pinched herself in masturbatory ecstasty. Naked from the waist down, Bret stepped closer to her. Taking the joint from her mouth, he took another hit, and held it in. Then, leaning forward to kiss her, he breathed smoke into her mouth. When he backed away, he handed her the roach, before peeling off his shirt and hoodie. His Ray Bans on. He made sure of that.

"Here, there's one or two more hits left," he said. He lifted Leather Boy's hips off of the floor, so that he was bent forward from the waist. "Any lube around here?"

Donna nodded, then pointed towards the bed. "Check that….thing over there. By the bed. There…should be some….Unnnnh….".

He couldn't read the label in the dark, but Bret

squirted some onto his stiff cock and some more onto his hand. The gel was cool, but Jonathan's asshole was warm. As he slathered the lube around this college kid's puckered asshole, Bret wondered if his fingernails were cut short enough. He stroked his huge cock with his hand, jerking it lazily to keep it stiff, while he inserted one index finger of his dominant hand into Leather Boy. The kid's sphincter muscles clenched and released around Bret's knuckle.

"Come on," Donna purred over her submissive's head, which was licking and lapping up her shaved pussy. "Just push that fucking snake of yours into him. I want to see you fuck my boy. Hard."

Bret lined himself up behind Jonathan's slender hips. Using his hand, he aimed the tip of his cock over the entrance of Leather Boy's little butthole, and then began to push. He pushed slowly–slowly, but with determination. He moaned, and lifted his head up from Donna's pussy.

"Ow," he screeched, "god-*damnit!*"

It was the first time Bret had heard Jonathan speak all night. *His voice is higher pitched than I would have thought,* he thought to himself.

Donna lifted up Leather Boy's head so that they were looking at one another. Her hand was like a vise around his face. "That feel good? Yeah? You like that?" He nodded, and then the Nurse gave him a little slap. She pushed him back down between her legs. "Good," she added. "Now get back to work."

Bret squeezed the kid's buttocks, then pulled Leather Boy's hips closer to him.

"Unnh," he said. "Fuck."

"How's that feel, Creep?"

He looked up. "He's really *tight,*" he told her. "Has he ever had a guy before?"

"Well, he told *me* he wasn't a virgin," she smiled, her teeth glowing in the near-darkness. "But I doubt whoever he was with had as big of a cock as *you.*"

Slowly, steadily, Bret began pumping his hips a bit more, his thick cock sliding just a little bit further up Jonathan's ass each time. The kid braced himself by pushing his palms up against the wall, on either side of Donna's hips. The Nurse's arms were toned and tense, and Bret felt Leather Boy starting to open up. Looking up at that filthy Nurse, he had to admit to his mostly-gay self that he found her confidence more than a little arousing. More than whether his partner had a cock or had a pussy, Bret got turned on by people who didn't give a fuck what other people thought. In this regard, Donna was a total fucking hottie. She could care less what other people thought of her.

She felt Bret looking at her, and she looked back. One was eating her out, while the other was riding his ass. The stranger with the Ray Bans was silently focused on his labor, a sheen of sweat beginning to appear on his chest and arms, glistening in the glow of the candle.

"That," she grunted. "That is so....fucking hot...".

Bret slapped Leather Boy's ass, trying to get deeper into him without increasing the pace. He reached down underneath, and found that the kid's cock was as hard as metal. Almost immediately after touching it, Jonathan squirted his spunk onto Bret's hand. He lifted his sticky fingers back up, then showed it to Donna.

"Gimme," she commanded.

Once he placed his cum-soaked fingers into her mouth, Bret began losing control of the rhythm. He began riding Leather Boy much harder now, galloping faster towards their irresistible destination, towards releasing into a really good fuck. Bret felt him his ass muscles clenching up, felt Jonathan tightening around his moving cock, and knew that they were close. Just a few more thrusts, and then he could unload.

"Don't come inside of him," Donna said, reading his mind. "Tell me just before you come, and then shoot it on me. I want it on my face."

Balancing now on just the balls of his feet, Bret was ramming all of his body weight into this little fuck boy, forcing Jonathan's to use his forearms against the wall now, his face all squashed up against Donna's stomach. Just before he came, when he felt that he couldn't hold it any longer, Bret pulled out. He jerked off the head of his cock, and looked at the Nurse.

"Aw shit," he said through clenched teeth, "it's gonna blow."

Donna quickly pushed Jonathan out of the way, who collapsed with a moan onto the floor. On her knees, Donna rubbed her clit furiously with one hand while she opened her mouth. Her tongue stuck out obscenely, wanting Bret to shoot his wad down her throat. She arched her back, offering all of herself to Bret, this stranger. She wanted him to humiliate her with his cum, and the anticipation of his ejaculate upon her skin made her grunt, like an animal in heat. When he finally shot onto her face, Donna spasmed. Her entire body convulsed, like she finally found relief from a deep and profound ache. Her hunger, at least for tonight, had finally been satiated.

Some of his come landed on her mouth. The rest, she smeared all over her skin–her cheeks and chin, down her throat and over her breasts. Donna made herself shiny in the dim light. Bret noticed there was no longer any music playing; when had the CD had stopped?

"Whew!" Donna leaned back, placing her bare ass on the floor against a nearby wall. Her legs were straight and splayed open in front of her, like some toy doll on a shelf, while Jonathan remained curled up on his side, in a fetal position. From the silence, the Nurse began to chuckle, a sound which grew in intensity and vibration from some-where deep down in her stomach.

"Holy shit," she yelled. "That was….just…what the doctor…ordered!"

"Glad to see this place hasn't changed that much," Bret said. "Hey. By the way: know where there's a phone I could use?

THE SURPRISE

I guess I should start my story at the Seaside, this restaurant along the Sound in Darien, Connecticut. Amber chose the place, and I remember it had a lot of outdoor seating. Even though the breeze blew pretty cool, they had thick blankets people could put over their laps to encourage folks to hang outside for people to eat, drink, and smoke. She had invited a bunch of people to meet us there, but we didn't want to tell them the "nature of the occasion". Let them guess, we thought. It wasn't either of our birthdays. Christmas was still a ways off. Folks probably thought we had gotten a dog or something, or maybe thought we were going to say we were going to move in together after we were done with college. A few—those that had known Amber the longest—were secretly hoping that at least one of us was going to announce finally getting a Real Job, something with steady income. Few were supportive of either of us continuing this ridiculous visual art (Amber) and writing (me) bullshit.

I don't think anybody seriously expected us to announce our engagement and intention to be married. That came as a real surprise.

Eight or nine people showed up, mostly from Amber's side: friends she grew up with, as well as some relatives. She grew up near here, in Rowayton, while everybody I knew were either in California or New York. Amber and I had met earlier this semester in Vermont, where both of us were in grad school; like most creative folks, the hope was that, after finishing our degrees, we could land a teaching gig somewhere to help support ourselves, keep making our art, and hopefully pay off all of the student loan debt. The MFA program at the college was pretty small, and both of us were about a decade older than the majority of the students on campus. Amber and I were basically loners, too, people who didn't really socialize much, only appearing in public when we needed to get more booze and drugs, or needed to get more coffee to keep working on whatever project we were making. I guess you could say we recognized a kindred spirit in one another, when we met during orientation, and quickly fell into a pattern that seemed to work well for both of us. When not in her studio collecting trash to add to the surface of her canvas to create her latest art project; and any time I left my desk, defeated, after spending hours banging on the keys of my laptop, Amber and I would meet up at her little cottage about a mile off campus. We'd start by talking about how our work was going, but it was a brief conversation. Usually, we'd start getting undressed as soon as possible. Looking back, the majority of the time Amber and I spent together wasn't spent in dialogue. Instead, the times we shared were primarily

about getting drunk or high, and then fucking each other
´s brains out.

Seriously. I´m not exaggerating. That's basically all
that we did. *Fuck.* We didn't go out to eat or see movies—
neither of us had a lot of money, anyway. Amber and I
tended to cook simple stuff at her place, then save up
whatever extra cash we had left over for used books, or
paint, or cheap booze, and whatever drugs we could
score. We could have gotten part-time jobs, of course, but
both of us had already done that while getting our Bache-
lors. Both Amber and I had saved up whatever money we
could so we could just focus on our Masters degree this
time, and not have to work at a job at the same time. I don
´t know. Looking back on it now, years later, maybe she
and I were just trying to appear more privileged than we
actually were. This college up in Vermont had a lot of
Trust Fund Babies, you know what I'm saying? I probably
sound like a snob, just for writing something like that
down, huh? Oh well.

On-campus, the student parties felt kind of silly for
both of us. Imagine being in high school, and being
invited to a party with a bunch of fourth-graders—it felt
like that. The main reason we went to Darien that particular weekend was to avoid this party on campus called the
"dress to get laid" party. All of the undergrads had been
talking it up all week. Neither Amber or myself knew
what the hell this party was all about, but it sounded
pretty lame and desperate. So, when Amber suggested we
go to Connecticut for the weekend and see her family, I
thought, what the hell, absolutely. Looking back on it, I
probably should've stayed on campus, pretended to be
sick. Something, anything other than going to Darien, and

doing what I did. I wish we would've just stayed in her cottage all weekend instead, fucking.

I'm using that word *fuck* intentionally by the way, and not just for shock value, or whatever. Amber and I didn't *make love*--we were never that soft or granola-crunchy with one another, during the few weeks we knew each other. I mean, sure: depending on who I was talking to–if I were "in polite company", or whatever–I would say that Amber and I *had sex.* But lots and lots of people just "have sex", and that doesn't quite capture the reality or the vibe of what Amber and I did. When we were together, Amber and I fucked. Hard. Passionately. Every moment we could get.

I'm not saying that what we were doing was healthy or anything, either. In fact, looking back with a tiny bit of maturity and perspective, I think the fucking was just an extention of the drinking and the drugs. All of it seemed to go together with Amber; each one felt interchangeable. Did Amber and I ever really talk about *anything*? Did we share anything important with one another? If we did, I can't remember it. It seemed like we were almost getting high or drunk. The few times we did interact without any substances inside our bodies–and with our clothes still on–was basically about scheduling. When are you coming over? Do you have any more weed? Shall I pick up some more liquor? When can we fuck again? Amber and I weren't "doing relationship", not in any conventional sense, anyway. But what we did have felt deeper than just being casual "fuck buddies" or "friends with benefits, too, yet far short of, like, *normal dating*. I don't know. Maybe we were just two feral creatures, trapped in a box that someone had kicked down the side of a mountain. Whatever I needed, Amber seemed to have it, or at least a piece of it. And, up until I joined her on the way to Darien that weekend, I seemed to have what she was looking for, too.

I'm probably over-analyzing this shit way too much.

We were a couple of addicts. Two broken toys trying to piece ourselves together, using whatever was available or nearby. We had bottomless holes inside that we were trying to fill with drinks, drugs, and fucking.

It all seemed like a good idea at the time.

AMBER and I were doomed from the start. On some reptilian brain level, we both knew that we were never going to last. Such connections like what we have burn bright but also burn brief. Neither of us had much of a plan besides getting high and fucking, and making some art once in a while.

So, of course, we got engaged.

Like everything else, that seemed like a good idea at the time, too.

This was our surprise, the reason why we had invited people to come out and meet us on such short notice at the Seaside. Did I even formally propose to Amber? I can't remember. Most likely, the plan to get engaged came up the night before, before driving to Connecticut. Maybe Amber thought we needed some sort of reason for visiting Darien in the middle of the semester? Couldn't just say, *Hey everybody! We're taking a break from that college you don't support me going to, because they're having this Dress to Get Laid Party. Can we crash here for the night?* But whatever. Amber had better success in assembling a group of people to show up for our impromptu engagement party. Like I said earlier, I didn't know anyone in Darien. I tried calling my friend Emilee, this visual artist from the college who I thought was pretty cool, but I couldn't reach her. I think she was busy finishing some kind of drawing project that weekend, or something.

Weather was bad as our car pulled out of the college parking lot and we drove out of Vermont. Heavy rain was beginning to fall, obscuring our vision and causing us to slow down. At one point, somewhere in Massachusetts, Amber pulled the car over to the side of the road. The road was really slick, and she wanted to wait until the rain lightened up before we continued driving. She used the buttons to roll down our windows just a crack before turning off the engine, while I rolled us a fresh joint. I got it lit and took the first hit, holding in the sweet bud, before passing the joint over. Amber adjusted the driver's seat so she could lean back, then propped her left foot onto the dash. I moved my seat back too, and looked at her through the smoke.

Amber's large green eyes, squinting while she squeezed another blast of smoke into her lungs, reminded me of an owl; they always seemed wide open, taking everything in at once. Her dark brown hair flowed long and straight, all the way down to her waist. Amber never did much in the way of exercise, but her limbs were strong and lean. She claimed she got this way from growing up by the water as a kid in Connecticut–swimming all the time, helping her dad work on his boat, stuff like that. After undergrad, she studied some kind of dance or performance art or something; she told me once, but I don't remember now. Basically, Amber didn't care how her body looked. For her, the body was a functional thing, and good enough so long as it did the things you wanted it to do.

We hung out in the car for a minute, passing the blunt back and forth, silently listening to the rain fall on the roof of her car. The pot was making both of us pleasantly high, and it seemed like she needed it a lot more than usual today. Amber took two drags each time she had it, and held in the smoke longer than she normally did. Was she nervous about this trip? Was something on her mind? She leaned forward to look at the rain falling down on the windshield.

"I think it's gonna be a while," she said, passing me the joint. Using her tongue and fingertips, she removed the bits of rolling paper that had stuck to her lips.

"That's cool," I nodded, smiling. "I'm good."

"Yeah?"

"Yeah. This is nice. Listening to the rain, and all."

She smiled, making a little sound in response. I guess I had given the correct answer to her unspoken question. Pulling a hair-band off of her wrist, Amber began gathering her hair up and behind her into a ponytail, before she began unbuttoning her shirt. None of her actions were seductive, but I got aroused watching her anyway. She wasn't really trying to tease me. Everything Amber did was a series of simple and necessary tasks, whose goal was always one thing: getting what she wanted.

"Unbutton your pants," she instructed quietly. I quickly unzipped, then lifted my hips off of the passenger seat so I could help a little bit as she pulled them down to the middle of my thighs. Before my ass had even touched back down onto the cold surface of the seat, Amber had shifted position on her side. Her legs were now folded underneath her, and her body was leaning forward towards me.

I was only half-hard when my cock entered her mouth, but it quickly got more stiff as she began to slurp. Amber made me feel like a teenager again, everything felt fast and always on the edge of exploding, and maybe this was the thing I miss the most about her–this raw sense of everything feeling urgent and new. Soon, I was gripping my butt muscles, trying to hold myself back from coming too soon. She sensed what I was up to, though, and lifted her head up to look at me.

"Don´t hold back," she grunted. Spit ran down her chin to the head of my dick, which she stroked with her right hand. She wiped the spit away with her tongue, licking around my shaft like she was enjoying an ice cream cone. "Come in my mouth. Please. I wanna swallow it."

Without waiting for any kind of answer, Amber swallowed me up again, and I groaned as my cock plunged deeper and further down into her throat. I writhed on top of the seat, watching her head bob up and down more rapidly, her strong lips wrapping around my shaft with just the right amount of friction. I arched my lower back while closing my eyes, afraid that if I kept looking at her that I would lose it. But both of us knew that I couldn't hold out for very long. And I wanted to see what she was doing, while she was doing it. Amber was so fucking hot. She was my favorite drug, the one that I couldn't ever imagine quitting.

"Oh fuck, oh fuck," I whined. I clutched the armrest below my window, leaving claw marks. Amber continued to suck vigorously, her throat making moaning sounds of encouragement, until I finally let it go inside her.

When I came, I could almost hear my come splash against the top of her throat. At least, I imagined I could. After I was finished, my dick began to go limp but remained even more sensitive, and Amber kept her mouth around me like she was riding a wild animal. Once my shuddering spasms died down, I moaned in total peace and joy. She looked up at me, wordlessly, tucking some of her long strands of hair behind an ear, then grinned as the tip of her tongue licked her top lip. Amber always caught every last drop. She sat back down in the driver's seat, happy as a cat who held a bird in its mouth. We looked through the wet windshield.

"It's stopped raining," she said, turning the key.

We didn't kiss each other, and she didn't wait for me to pull my pants up or fasten my seatbelt. According to the clock on the dash, we were going to be late to our own engagement party in Connecticut, if we didn't hurry up and get out of Massachusetts.

"YOU TWO ARE GETTING *MARRIED*?"

Barbara tried to conceal the concern spreading across her face, trying desperately to force the muscles around her mouth into something resembling a smile of support. That evening at the Seaside was the first time I was meeting Amber's mom—well, stepmom. Actually, Barbara *used* to be her stepmom, when Amber's father Jack was married to her, from when Amber was ten and through the end of high school. Crucial years. Obviously, Barbara looked nothing like her former-stepdaughter. In contrast to Amber's androgynous body and long brown hair, Barbara's hair was short and blonde, with a torso broad in the back (from lifting weights) and full in the front (from cosmetic surgery). Her teeth were blindingly bright, but her eyes remained dull when she spoke to me. "Congratulations," she said, after a pause that everyone noticed but all tried not to call attention to.

"Yeah, man," Lawson said, slapping me on the back. "Right on!" He was the only person I knew there, someone who was in one of Amber's nude modeling classes up in Vermont. Did he drive all the way down here? I had seen him around campus, but never had a conversation with him. I think his father worked for some big pharmaceutical company or something. A Trust Fund Kid. "This is a celebration," he continued. "Let me buy you all the first round. What are we drinking?"

"Thanks," Amber said. "How about…..Long Island Ice Teas!"

Lawson's eyes glowed with glee at her suggestion, while Barbara blinked repeatedly like she had just seen a small animal get run over by a car. "Perfect," he clapped. "Be right back."

Turning back towards my finacé, I saw that a handful of people had encircled Amber, wanting to catch up. I didn't know any of them. I drifted towards the doors which opened onto the restaurant's deck, savoring the cool breeze coming off of the Sound and debating whether I should have a cigarette or not. I had never met Amber's friends from where she grew up before, but even with our announcement they did little more than provide a handshake or a clap on the back, before turning back to her. Like Barbara, her friends assessed my value (or lack thereof) instantly, just from looking at me. My clothes were old and worn down. Like Amber, I was also an artist–though who really wanted to devote their lives to becoming a *writer*, for fuck´s sake? But unlike Amber, I didn't have any history with these people. Exhaling, I turned my back to the interior of the restaurant and leaned on the edge of the brass rail. I was rubbing my eyes when Lawson returned, placing a Long Island Iced Tea into my hand.

"Here you go, man," he said, clinking my glass. "And many more!"

Drinks. Drinks, and more drinks. With each round, more sloshed around inside my head instead of my belly. Time quickly got fuzzy around the edges, and it appeared as though Lawson was making it his personal mission to get me good and drunk. *When was the last time I ate?* I vaguely remember making a clumsy trip towards the men's room, and nearly falling into the chest of one of Amber´s friends along the way. *Did I spill a drink into her lap?* The room was spinning too fast to tell. I had never had a Long Island Iced Tea before that night, only learning later that the drink contains five different kinds of alcohol. Jesus!

Wobbling back from taking a piss, I tried concentrating on my steps. I wanted to prove that I wasn't *that* wasted. Barbara was talking with Amber at a table, and looking around, it seemed that we were the only ones left. Even Lawson had left the Seaside for something more interesting than watching me get smashed, I guess. How long had I been in there? Amber leaned closer to her former- stepmom, whose forehead wrinkled into a frown.

I bumped into a wooden stool, and when she looked up, I didn't recognize my fiancé for a second. Instead of a smile, which is how she usually greeted me, all I saw there now was disgust. Her face was that of somebody who realized they had just made a big mistake.

THE SHORT DRIVE back to Barbara´s house in Darien was rough, between the silence in the car and the pain of my splitting headache. Amber and I had accepted her former-stepmom´s invitation to spend the night there, instead of driving back to Vermont that same night. I'm grateful that she seemed to believe that at least one of us was sober enough to drive ten minutes, back to her house. I felt afraid to look at Amber for too long, though, during the drive. Her lips kept chewing on something unseen, while the rest of her body remained motionless leaning towards the driver's seat window as we made our way through to the Darien suburbs. Obviously, something was occupying her mind, but so far, she wasn't letting me in on what it was. And I was afraid to ask.

When Amber pulled her car into the driveway, Barbara´s silver Range Rover was already there. Without a word, Amber got out of the car and walked to the fence, walking along the two-story house towards the back. Her former- stepmother´s yard was huge, filled with tall trees and manicured bushes. She even had a hot tub. In one corner of the yard was a tiny guest cottage with its porchlight on, which is where I assumed the two of us were going to sleep. However, Amber took a left turn to enter through a sliding glass door, before climbing up two stairs at a time to the second floor. Generous of Barbara, I thought, letting us sleep in the house. Maybe everything wasn't as bad as I thought? Maybe everything was okay, and I was just being paranoid earlier, because of the booze. Maybe this hospitality was her former-stepmom's way of saying she approved of Amber's engagement announcement?

When I reached the top of the stairs, I stepped into the hallway bathroom, as those drinks were still running through me. When I found Amber, she was opening a second-story window inside a sparsely-furnished room. The breeze felt frosty in here, and blew against the thin white curtains like sails of a ship. At her feet on the floor were twenty or thirty candles, arranged in a crude semi-circle near a yoga mat. She was lighting each one with a lighter, ignoring my appearance. A good-size mattress lay on the floor, its sheets crisp, and a layer of clear plastic was crumpled beside it. One wall was light blue, but the others were white. A stack of paint cans and some brushes were piled in a neat corner on the other side.

When she finished with the candles, Amber undressed. I felt invisible, or that I didn't even count, just like when we were at the Seaside; my fiancé was acting as though I wasn't even there. After unbuttoning her shirt, she turned her back to me before pulling it over her head, as if she didn't want me looking at her. Her bare back was bisected by a small black sports bra, and she took her time folding the shirt neatly into a square before moving on to her pants. The silence from the car ride home, plus the freeze-out in this strange new house, was needling me. In retrospect, I wish I had just kept my mouth shut.

"Hey. Hey, babe," I began tentatively, trying to sound casual. "What's going on? Did I do something?"

She turned around swiftly. The candles illuminated her skin with an eerie Halloween-like glow, her half naked body only visible in silhouette. Even in the semi-darkness, though, I could tell that her eyes were burning red.

"How much did you drink?"

Her simple question was laced with accusation. Amber and I been drinking and fucking and getting high together as a matter of course for these past few months, but neither of us had ever brought up *how much* we did. Before we were engaged, I guess. Up until tonight, that was an unwritten rule between us. How much we took to get high was just our own business. Or maybe she was realizing that what was normal up in Vermont looked more than a little fucked up down here in Connecticut.

"I don´t know," I said, trying my best to keep my eyes up. "What does it matter? Two or three...?"

"Six," she shouted. "You had *six* of those goddamn Long Island Ice Teas!"

I jerked my head back in confusion. "So what? It was a celebration! People wanted to buy us drinks for our engagement," I said, tentatively coming closer to her. "Lawson was happy to–."

"Lawson didn't pay for all of those," she said, slapping my hand away. "My Mom did!"

"Wait. Barbara did?" I frowned. I hadn't realized. My first time meeting her former-stepmom, and I was not only coming off as some poor hack, but as a total drunk, too. Great. That's just great.

"Aw, fuck. I´m sorry, babe. Hey, Amber. Amber?" I

moved closer to her tiny frame. This time, she let me put my hands on her bare back. I resisted moving them down to her waist, and instead just contented myself with kissing the top of her head. Her hair smelled faintly of marijuana. We stood and breathed together in the room for a bit, and eventually I felt her hands wrap around me. I moved my hands down to feel the strong cords of Amber's muscles just above her waist, and just kept them there, waiting. When we moved our heads away from one another, and I looked into her face, I could see that her big owl-like eyes were softer now. At least, I thought so. Hoped so. It was hard to be sure, with the dim lighting. Her torso trembled beneath my touch.

"I just," she sniffled, then took a deep breath in. "I just wanted this night to be...good. Perfect."

"Hey," I said, lifting up her chin. "It *is* good! The night is still young. Let's just, you know, start over."

She wiped her eyes, then looked back at me while she shook her head. "But you had so much to *drink.*"

"Hey, hon," I said. "I wanna make it up to you. What can I do?"

Amber raised an eyebrow, then put one hand on my crotch, gently squeezing and rubbing me there. "Hi," she whispered playfully. "Can we....celebrate?"

I took a deep breath in, feeling myself growing harder and harder from her touch. "I think...you know...the answer to *that.*"

My crooked grin vanished with her kiss. She kept her hand stroking me between my legs for a while, until she pressed her hips into mine. Amber's torso was smooth and supple, and our kiss activated more heat within the cold new room. My tongue darted and swirled inside her wet mouth, and my hands explored the different contours of her back–all the little ridges between her vertebrae, the muscular columns of her postural muscles, the soft triangles of her shoulder blades. Her hands gripped my waist, pulling me closer to her, before she started frantically untucking my shirt from my waist. I pulled away from the kiss for a moment, trying to help get my goddamn shirt off as quickly as possible. Amber began working on the belt of my jeans.

"This has to go," she whispered matter of factly.

I peeled off my shirt and tossed it into a dark corner of the room, while Amber tugged my pants and underwear down to my ankles. I tried to help, doing a small march in place with my feet, but that actually just got me tangled up further, my clothes now inside-out around my ankles. I chuckled, but Amber remained focused and intent on stripping me down, pronto. Using her hands, she moved each of my legs up, one at a time, to remove the pant legs, until only my socks remained. Finished with her first task, she looked at my cock while she spoke.

"I need it, Daddy," she purred. "Can I have it?"

Before I could say anything, Amber had swallowed me whole. She slowly brought her warm wet mouth down to the base of my shaft, causing a moan to rip free of my lips. My eyelids fluttered as I looked down at her, and then I arched my face up towards the ceiling as she began to suck me, back and forth.

Most of the time, I didn´t like to talk during sex. I hardly made any sound at all, really. But Amber? She liked to talk dirty, and especially enjoyed calling me *Daddy* when we fucked. Calling me that turned her on, which then turned *me* on, so it was a win-win. I remember asking her about it once, early on in our relationship.

"Why do you call me *Daddy* when we´re, like…you know?"

"You mean, when we´re *fucking*?"

"I was going to say *having sex,* but yeah, sure, *fucking* is probably a more accurate word to describe what we do."

"I agree."

"….So? You gonna answer the question?"

"What? You don't like it when I call you *Daddy*?"

"I didn't say *that.* I was just curious why you like calling me that. I mean, do you have… *Daddy issues,* or something?"

"No, asshole, I don't have *Daddy issues*. I just…like saying it sometimes."

"Uh huh."

"And…I can see that you…like it, too."

I looked back down. Kneeling on the floor, Amber´s slender legs were cushioned from the hardwood floor by the edge of the yoga mat. She was sucking me really vigorously, and I felt I might lose my balance if I stayed standing up. Another breeze blew in through the windows, causing the skin on my chest to form goose-bumps. I shivered, and then gently moved my cock out of her mouth.

"Okay," I panted, "my turn."

When Amber came back onto her feet, the movement of her slender limbs reminded me of a doe rising up from the ground. Her bare chest was almost boyish, her nipples large and her breasts small. The muscles of her stomach were defined, and her breath was panting in and out from the effort and the longing. We came together again for a brief and sloppy kiss, holding each other tight for a moment, before she stepped back. She smoothly dropped her pants off of her body now, her bare hips not wearing any underwear. Holding my hand, Amber guided us to the mattress behind her, propping herself up on her elbows. After I yanked my feet free of the socks, she opened her bent legs in invitation.

I crawled towards her, eager to please. Bending my elbows, I placed my mouth on the inside of her leg, right around the knee joint. I first wanted to tease her a little, show her that I was still someone worthwhile, someone who knew how to fuck and have fun. That she hadn't made any mistakes with me. Maybe she would tell her friends and even Barbara about this later, how we had kissed and made up after coming back from the Seaside. Maybe everyone would forget about my drunken behavior earlier tonight. I smiled at the fantasy, making a little trail of kisses along her inner thigh, her pubic hair tickling the side of my cheek. Amber squirmed her hips closer to my mouth, her pelvis making tiny circles and figure-eights, but I wanted her to yearn for it just a little while longer. Then, I moved my kisses over to the inside of her other leg, right around the knee, and continued taking my time before bringing my mouth towards her wet pussy.

"You bastard," she said, with a chuckle. "You want me to beg?"

Without lifting my lips from her body, I murmured yes, before surrendering to her wishes. Placing my lips just above glistening folds, I stuck out my tongue, tracing the outside of her full, dark pink lips. She pushed her pelvis towards me, and I began to lick and suck, lapping up every drop of her. I consumed her, listening to her body language, her sounds, trying to sense what she wanted more of. Sometimes, I would linger here, stay longer there, giving her what she wanted; other times I would change the rhythm, withdraw and pull away, keep her on her toes. Through all of her moans, I could feel her sex vibrating all the way down into her hips and into my face.

"Don´t stop," she whispered urgently. "Don´t stop."

Amber cradled the back of my skull, using her hands to push my head further into her. Her hips began quaking beneath my mouth, and I moved my jaw faster. She was close, and I was determined to make my fiancé come first.

"Ahhh-ungggh-AHHHH!" Her voice squealed with pleasure, and her body quivered against me like lightning. Usually, Amber was unapologetically loud when we fucked, but tonight she was probably trying to keep a lid on it because of her mom-slash-stepmom-slash whomever outside the open window, down in the guest cottage.

She was still coming down from her orgasm when I climbed forward for another sloppy kiss. The front of my face was drenched with her juices, but neither of us gave a fuck. Our tongues slithered inside one another´s mouths, searching for more of something neither of us could put a name to. When her hands found my cock and began stroking it, I broke away from our kiss, and Amber immediately rolled over onto her elbows and knees. She wiggled her ass left and right in my face a little, teasing me. I knelt on the edge of the mattress, and then just took a moment to gaze down at her perfect round ass.

Amber´s upper torso might have been boyish, a series

of vertical and horizontal lines, but her hips were all wondrous curves, and her ass a perfect orb cleft in the middle like a luscious piece of fruit. My cock grew hard just looking at her, and I placed my palms reverently on top of her firm butt. I used my thumbs to slowly spread her cheeks apart so I could better aim the head of my dick into her warm and wet pussy. I slid in easily. Our pubic bones gently slammed up against each other's, and both of us groaned. If Barbara hadn't heard us fucking before, she definitely was going to now, along with every one of her neighbors in this cul-de-sac. Amber was so fucking hot, and tonight the sex was feeling really fucking good. Like we were mending something, with the sex, or at least trying to repair whatever it was I had torn up earlier at the Seaside. I felt invincible now: powerful, on top of the world. I gave her ass a slap, and Amber instantly began bucking her tight little ass cheeks up against me.

"That's it, Daddy," she said. She looked over her shoulder at me, her eyelids heavy in the flickering candle-light. "Give it to me."

I had never slapped her ass before, but clearly she was into it. So, I slapped her ass again. I was getting quickly aroused by how dirty this felt, how we were becoming more and more animal, de-evolving. Amber, *my fucking fiancé,* began pumping and pushing her hips into me. Her torso was lean and strong, and beads of perspiration were glistening along the tiny ravines and crevices of her back. And then, just when I felt like I couldn't take it anymore, she began moving faster. She was really pounding into me, getting real nasty. Her body pushed me closer and closer towards making me come, but I didn't want to do that just yet. I gave her ass another slap, this one harder than the others. I wanted to show her that I could be in charge, that I could be a real man for her. A *good husband.* That I wasn't some kind of a mistake, someone she needed to be ashamed of.

Amber kept working her body up against mine, so I slapped her ass again. Hard enough this time to make sure I had her attention.

"Slow down, bitch," I said.

I meant it to be funny, I think. Or sexy. I wanted to talk dirty, like she did all the time. But I don't know. Whatever I was trying to do, it didn't go the way I wanted it to. Suddenly, the hot sexual energy in the room turned to ice, and Amber seemed less into what we were doing, as if I had just punctured the air out of a tire. Everything she was doing now was mechanical, silent. Something inside of her had just flown out the window; it's like I could almost see it. She looked over her shoulder at me again, but this time her eyes were sharp instead of soft.

"Don't call me that."

"I'll call you whatever I want, bitch," I said. "Come on. Work that fucking ass."

Even as I slapped her ass again, I knew I shouldn't have said that. Should've kept my big mouth shut. Should have stopped trying to prove anything, should've not pretended to be anything other than what I was. Instead of stopping, it was like I was doubling-down, becoming the thing she specifically asked me *not* to be. Instead of stopping, I just said it again, and with an attitude.

It seemed like a good idea at the time.

I slapped Amber's ass again, harder than ever. Looking back on it now, I can see that I was chickenshit: afraid of talking to her; afraid that we wouldn't have sex ever again if we stopped right then; afraid that she was realizing that I was the last person she should be engaged to. Afraid of letting her see me, really see me, even though we had been fucking for over two months now.

Afraid she would leave me.

Jesus fucking Christ. Some engagement party, huh?

In front of me, Amber brought her upper body down onto the mattress along her forearms, her head and face vanishing beneath her long brown hair. She looked like she had given up. The sex felt increasingly one-sided now, like she was just waiting for me to hurry up and finish. But, like the fucking genius that I am, I didn't stop. No words now. Silver lining. That, and I was no longer slapping her ass. Or calling her my bitch. We had stopped fucking already, but our bodies hadn't woken up to the fact yet.

I kept pumping my cock into her pussy, desperate. I wanted to go back in time, have a chance to do it all over. Even without much love or intimacy between us, we used to have fun with each other. We were like drinking buddies, but just with a lot of sex thrown in. For a couple months, we were able to help each other turn off the noise of the outside world. But not anymore. Now, tonight, I was the noise that she was to get away from. And me? I was the guy who keeps drinking even when he doesn't feel the booze anymore. Doesn't feel *anything* anymore. *Drinking myself straight.*

I don't know what Amber and me were doing now, but it definitely wasn't having sex anymore. She just lay there with her ass up in the air like a zombie, or a goddamn ragdoll, or whatever. I was still moving my hips back and forth, under the delusion that it would somehow all get better, that somehow my *cock* would bring us back to whatever kind of normalcy we had before Darien. *The arrogance of that.* But Amber: she was just *there*–her beautiful hips were still there, up in the air. And she was letting me pound her beautiful pussy. But she was not giving very much back.

And that pissed me off.

I grabbed some of Amber's long hair and pulled. I shouldn't have done that, I know; especially after all the other crap I had put her through tonight. Why the hell *did* I do that? Maybe on some level I figured, *Hey, you're already being a total dick, why stop* now? *Does anything even matter anymore?* Pulling her hair, I forced her back up on her palms again, her spine arched and curved now. I used my other hand to pull her hips tighter to mine, so I could thrust deeper into her lifeless pussy. Trying to make something out of nothing. I felt like I was trapped in a role in a movie I didn't want to be in, pretending to be someone else. Or maybe this *was* the real me: maybe this was the first time I was truly naked, and letting Amber see the real me. See the guy she had gotten engaged to.

"Come on, bitch," I growled. "Take it."

Amber didn't say anything. What was the point? What was she going to say? And when I finally came a few seconds later, it felt hollow. Empty. I felt incredibly alone. In the past, both of us would moan or scream or yell together when one of us had an orgasm. Those times, it felt like both of us were releasing something together, getting closer to one another. But not tonight. Tonight, after I came, I just grunted, feeling self-conscious and ashamed.

Our fucking used to have the power to make everything better. Now, it just made everything wrong.

Panting, sweaty, depressed, I lay down onto my back next to her, furthest from the open window. Should I touch her? No. My touch was some kind of grease. Amber was curled up into a ball facing away from me, the blanket already covering her body up to her ears.

"Hey babe," I said. "You gonna blow out the candles?"

She didn't say anything. I placed a hand on her shoulder, and she shivered. I moved my hand away.

Fuck.

I tried to think of something to say. We should talk, work this out. Ask her how she is feeling? No, that would just make her more upset, as I already knew what she was feeling. Maybe I should just apologize. But for which part? Drinking at the Seaside? Slapping her ass? Calling her a bitch? Entering her life in the first place? Going to college in Vermont?

My mind began to drift. I had had so much booze that night, and I felt like I was being caught in its undertow. Fucking Long Island Iced Teas. I tried lifting my head, blow out the candles. We shouldn't leave them burning all night. We needed to blow them out. But I was so tired. I couldn't move my legs, or keep my head up. I couldn't keep my eyes open...

I stopped fighting. The waters of oblivion rushed over my head and sucked me down, dragging me to the thick darkness of unconsciousness. I didn't put up any kind of a fight.

Amber and I would talk in the morning. When we were both sober, fresh. I'd make us some coffee, and we'd take a walk. We'd figure something out.

Everything would be okay...in the morning...

SWEAT. Heat. Wake up. *Wake up!*

I wake up. Sweating. I´m hot. I was drifting into the blackout but now I feel hot. Something woke me and my reptile brain up. Cold, earlier. Now, hot. Where was the breeze?

Eyes, open. Turn my head. Amber. Curled up, in a ball, facing me, eyes closed.

Behind her, flames.

The corner of the bedroom was completely engulfed in fire.

"Holy shit!"

The curtains. One of the candle flames must have caught the bottom of one, igniting a sail of fire. And so fast! The flames were licking the walls in a hungry ball of orange and red and blue. How long had we been sleeping here?

Coughing, I violently shook Amber´s shoulder.

"Amber! *Amber!*"

She wasn't opening her eyes. Had she inhaled too much smoke already? The temperature in the room was increasing by the second. We had to get out of here.

"Amber, wake up," I shouted. "Amber!"

She opened her eyes groggily. For a second, her eyes looked upon me in a soft focus, tenderly. Then she remembered that she hated my guts. Then she coughed, her eyes watering as she looked towards the walls of flame. She froze in fear, a deer in the headlights. But goddamn if I was going to screw one more thing up tonight.

"Amber, *FIRE*," I yelled. "Get out of here!"

She leapt out of bed, naked. The air grew thick with smoke, the flames surrounding the window, engulfing where the curtains used to be. The rubber edges of the yoga mat curled up and made the smoke smell funny. Amber's shirt was nowhere to be found, but I tossed her pants at her like a baseball pitcher.

"Run," I yelled. "Get Barbara!"

Her feet ran downstairs while I pulled the thick blanket from the bed. I tried snuffing out the flames by hitting it with the blanket, trying to take away the oxygen, like I saw on TV shows as a kid. But all *I* was doing, here in real life, was making things worse. As usual. The fire now burned the edges of the blanket. I tried to hit the corner where the source of the fire was, but I just ended up spreading the flames around the room faster.

Jesus, can't I do anything fucking right?

I heard the sound of sirens from outside, and so I gave up. The smoke was getting thick in there, and it was getting hard to see. I was halfway down the stairs when I realized I forgot my clothes upstairs. I looked back up, but the doorway of the bedroom was just all fire now. I raced downstairs, naked, and into the front yard.

Outside, Barbara and Amber stood watching the burning house that I had just emerged from. Barbara had a cell phone curled in her hand, held close to her chest like a talisman. Amber wore my shirt, and had one of her arms wrapped around her former-stepmom's solid body. Their faces just looked up at the second story of the house, as it all went up in flames. Neither acknowledged

113

me, as I stood there. Neither cared that I was naked and cold, or that I was alive.

"Come on, come on, come on," Barbara kept whispering to herself. The sirens grew louder, closer, and seemed to be coming from the south.

I didn't know what to do, but I was freezing, so I ran along the side of the burning house and into Barbara's guest cottage, and pulled the first thing I saw: a hand-knitted blanket that was draped over a chair near the door. It looked like something your grandma made for you as a house-warming gift. It didn't cover my entire body, but at least I felt I could try to get a little warm. My legs and arms were still bare, but it covered most of my upper back like a poncho. When I returned out front, three fire trucks were there, and a fireman was waving Barbara and Amber towards him. He was yelling at them to move further away from the house. They ran into the middle of the street, and I followed. I didn't know where else to go, or what to do. The fireman who had motioned to them looked surprised to see me. Then he just told me to hurry up, in a tone of voice like he didn't care if I did or not. Like I was an idiot.

The two women stood motionless in the middle of the street. Barbara spoke with another fireman, while the others attached hoses to the hydrant, hoping to douse it and salvage as much of the house that they could, stop it from spreading into the rest of the houses on the block. I walked barefoot into the street to join Amber, the gravel hurting the bottoms of my feet with every step. Her face turned blue and red from the lights of the trucks.

"Whoa," I said, putting my hand on her shoulder. "Are you okay, hon?"

My voice must have snapped her out of her trance, because she looked over at me as if for the first time. There was no tenderness there. And there never would be, ever again. Amber was disgusted.

"You burned down my mother's house."

"What? No, I–".

"Fucking asshole," she said, shaking her head and turning back to look at the house. "Just get out of my face."

"Amber, what? Honey, I just–."

"I said, *get–the fuck–out of here!*"

Barbara looked over at us for a moment, then turned back to the fireman. She had more important things to take care of, and she knew her daughter could handle a fuck-up like me. Another member of the crew approached, and used his body to create a shield between Amber and me.

"Are you okay, miss?"

I tried to step around the guy, but the fireman's gloved hand swatted me away.

"Hey, what the fuck," I said. "That's my fiancé–."

"You best just calm down there, son," he said. He looked me in the eye, and his lip twitched. Without using any words, I knew exactly what would happen to me if I were to say another word, do anything besides breathe. I nodded my understanding. He turned back to Amber, said something I couldn't hear, then gave me a final look before getting back to something important. He helped two others unspool a second hose.

I tried to tighten the blanket around my naked body, and cried. If I wasn't such a coward, I would have run back into the house, let myself burn up. I kept hoping for

115

Amber to say something, or just look at me. Anything. But she just stepped forward, watching the men do their jobs and put out that fire. With that one step, I had become invisible. Nothing. A big fat zero.

How long did I stand there? I don't know. Eventually, though, I turned away, and walked away from the burning house. Nobody wanted me there. Nobody needed me. I was a waste of space. Amber and I never spoke again.

I sat down across the street, thinking, waiting for the flames to turn into smoke. Eventually morning came, and someone let me use their phone, someone let me borrow some used clothes. But everything was over a long time before that.

OTHER BOOKS BY CHRISTIAN PAN

City of Desire

https://www.amazon.com/dp/B0BLKZF78L

Short stories by Christian Pan

SEASON'S TEASINGS: A SEXY HOLIDAY COLLECTION

(ed. by Olivia Lawless)

ACKNOWLEDGMENTS

Writing and rewriting is an individual art that I am fortunate to do within an incredible community. As always, I would like to thank Tim, whose writing workshops taught me invaluable tools to bring my writing to completion; Cheyann, for recognizing that I was a writer of erotica before I did; Chris, Michael, Amanda, Matt, Rebecca, Kevin, Dan, Missy, Tony, Tori, and Karen for immediately getting the book; everyone in the Queer Erotic Content Creators Club, for your support; Dan, for the website; Emilee, for her beautiful visual art which accompanied some of these stories when they were first published; Tatiana, for showing me how to jazz up a book cover; Megan L, for excellent feedback and criticism; the and Megan D., my indefatigable champion.

ABOUT THE AUTHOR

Christian Pan is a bisexual writer based in New York City who writes original and customized erotic fiction. He has published over 80 short stories in English, Spanish, and French. His writing appears in *Season's Teasings: A Sexy Holiday Collection* (edited by Olivia Lawless). His first book, *City of Desire,* was published in November 2021.

For more information: www.christianpanerotica.com.

Made in the USA
Columbia, SC
29 January 2023

10660339R00070